THE JAPA

Susannah met and fell in love with Fernando
Cuevas in London. She little thought when
she travelled out to Spain to work for a
wealthy family that the child she had come
to teach was Fernando's child and that she
would be meeting Fernando himself far
sooner than she had expected . . .

Books you will enjoy
by ANNE MATHER

WITCHSTONE
When Ashley's father died she travelled northwards
to make her home with her uncle and aunt in their
small hotel. While helping there she met Jake, a man
of undeniable attraction for her, but one who had
to be remote for many reasons – but most of all
because of his forthcoming marriage to Barbara ...

DARK MOONLESS NIGHT
Seven years ago Caroline had considered Gareth
Morgan unsuitable as a husband for herself. Now
they met again in the African jungle and Caroline's
feelings had changed. But the disturbing Gareth
told her, 'If you have any foolish notion of
entertaining yourself while you're here by trying to
rekindle old fires, you'll be wasting your time!'
What should she do?

RACHEL TREVELLYAN
The arrogant Luis Martinez, Marqués de Mendao,
made it clear that all he felt for Rachel was
contempt. Did it matter that she seemed unable to
convince him that he was wrong about her? And
what about Malcolm's feelings?

SILVER FRUIT UPON SILVER TREES
It would be easy, Eve told Sophie. All she had to
do was to go to Trinidad and pretend to be the
granddaughter of the wealthy Brandt St. Vincente
for four weeks and the money she needed would be
hers. But when Sophie met the disturbing Edge St.
Vincente, who thought she was his niece, and fell in
love with him, she realized that perhaps it wasn't
going to be that simple after all ...

THE JAPANESE SCREEN

by

ANNE MATHER

MILLS & BOON LIMITED
17–19 FOLEY STREET
LONDON W1A 1DR

First published 1974
This edition 1974

© *Anne Mather 1974*

ISBN 0 263 71707 0

Made and Printed in Great Britain by
Cox & Wyman Ltd, London, Reading and Fakenham

CHAPTER ONE

FERNANDO hadn't wanted to come to the party. Parties were not his favourite form of relaxation and after the hectic negotiations of the past few days that was what he most needed. But the Castanas were friends of the family, and he could hardly have refused Lucie's invitation without causing a rift in relationships. All the same, after over an hour of small talk, of circulating in a smoke-filled room and making conversation out of a multitude of inane pleasantries, he was more than ready to leave. He was tired and not in the best of tempers, and he was growing weary of Lucie's determined attempts to flirt with him. She was a married woman with a child, and should have been beyond such a thing. Certainly in Spain her behaviour would have caused a number of raised eyebrows and the kind of gossip no self-respecting woman would want to arouse. But apparently Lucie imagined herself far from the rigid ethics of her own country, and as her husband was away for a few days on business, she was surrendering to the somewhat permissive society of London.

He looked round the crowded lounge wondering what excuse he could give for leaving so early. By no means were all the people present Spaniards. It was true that a large percentage were fellow compatriots, but the Castanas numbered English and Americans among their friends, too. There was a plentiful supply of wines and spirits, should he have felt so inclined, and an excellent buffet occupied the long tables to one side of the room. A hi-fi system offered an undistracting mixture of popular music and he supposed that of its type it was a reasonably successful gathering. But the truth was he was bored, and he thought with a sense of resignation that the isolation of his study back home would have offered a more than adequate substitute.

'Fernando?'

Lucie was offering him yet another cocktail which he politely refused, summoning his determination to apologize and take his leave, when there was an unexpected interruption of the proceedings. A small boy came careering into the room, looking round a trifle desperately for a familiar face. When he saw Lucie he made straight for her, clinging to her skirts and crying wildly. He was wearing only pyjama trousers and as his face and hands were most obviously wet and possibly sticky, Lucie, not unnaturally, tried to push him away from her. But the boy cried all the louder and a ripple of amused speculation ran round the room.

A girl was following the boy, Fernando saw now, and she had halted rather uncertainly at the door to the crowded lounge. Then, with a slight shrug of her shoulders, she moved towards the boy and his mother. She was embarrassed, no doubt conscious of the conspicuousness of her blue nylon overall beside so many extravagant evening creations, and Fernando felt an unexpected stirring of sympathy. Women, young or old, did not particularly interest him, but this slender girl, a little above average height with dark-fringed eyes and a mass of ash-blonde hair that was presently secured rather inadequately by two elastic bands, aroused his compassion.

'What do you think you are doing, Eduardo?' Lucie was demanding in English for the benefit of their guests. 'You know you are not permitted to come in here in the evenings. Señorita King!' She turned on the girl. 'What is the meaning of this?'

The girl's cheeks were pink, but she took a firm hold on the boy's hand before replying. 'I'm sorry, *señora*. Eduardo has been unwell, and he insisted upon seeing you. I told him you could not be disturbed, but he ran away from me.'

Lucie clearly couldn't decide whether or not to rail at the girl there and then or retire gracefully and make her feelings known at some future date. However, her Latin temperament seemed to get the better of discretion, because in heated tones she exclaimed: 'What do you mean – he ran away from you? What were you doing,

6

señorita? Are you not capable of controlling one small boy?'

The girl stood her ground, and Fernando admired her for it. 'Eduardo and I were in the bathroom trying to get him cleaned up,' she declared. 'He slipped out of the door when my back was turned. I followed as quickly—'

Lucie waved her hands impatiently. 'Spare me these small details, *señorita*,' she snapped. 'You know perfectly well that while his father is away Eduardo is inclined to be a little – er – upset.'

The girl listened and then said quietly, but distinctly: 'I think the amount of sweets he consumed this afternoon is a more likely explanation, *señora*—'

Lucie clasped her hands together. 'That will do, *señorita*,' she interrupted her shrilly. 'I will not be argued with in this insolent manner—'

'Lucie! Cool down!' Fernando spoke to her in their own language. 'There is no harm done.' He glanced in the girl's direction and met her level gaze, noting that she did not seem to welcome his intervention, but going on in spite of it. 'Er – Señorita King is not to blame. Eduardo is young – he is impulsive. He naturally wanted to be with you – he wanted your love and attention when he was feeling unwell.'

Lucie measured his gaze for a long moment and then he saw the unwelcome invitation appear in her eyes again. 'Yes – yes. You are right, Fernando,' she agreed, responding in an intimate patois. She turned back to her son and his companion. 'You may go along with Señorita King, Eduardo. We will say no more about this tonight.' She shifted her gaze to encompass the girl. 'We will discuss it further in the morning—'

But now Eduardo was hanging back, tugging at the girl's hand, looking imploringly at his mother, then at Fernando. 'I want to stay, Mama,' he whimpered. 'Do not send me away!'

Fernando stepped forward, squatting down beside the boy, smiling at him encouragingly. 'Your mama is busy right now, Eduardo. As you can see, she has guests to attend to. Tomorrow she will have time for you.'

7

'Tomorrow she will be tired,' accused Eduardo tearfully. 'And Papa is away . . .'

Fernando hesitated. He had no wish to get further involved with the Castanas, but Eduardo's forlorn face aroused his sympathy. 'I have an idea,' he said gently. 'Tomorrow I shall not be busy – or tired. How would you like me to come and take you – where?' He shrugged. 'The park – the zoo?'

Eduardo's face lit up. 'I have not been to the zoo,' he exclaimed.

'The zoo it is, then. Tomorrow morning at – let me see – ten o'clock?' He raised his eyes to the girl's face, and speaking in English said: 'Eduardo and I are going to the zoo. Will tomorrow at ten be suitable?'

The girl inclined her head and looked to Lucie for guidance. 'I – I suppose so.'

'That is so kind of you, Fernando,' exclaimed Lucie, as he straightened. 'Eduardo misses a man's attention.' She smiled, and her eyes said: *As I do myself*, but Fernando chose to ignore it.

'Very well.' Fernando was speaking in English again now. 'Good-bye for the present, Eduardo.'

'*Adios, señor!*' Eduardo's face was wreathed in smiles and he went with the girl quite happily then.

The girl herself walked away with a certain amount of unconscious dignity, and watching her straight back Fernando wondered why he had bothered to intervene on her behalf. He had not done it for Lucie's sake, to prevent her from making a fool of herself in front of her guests, he had wanted to save the girl – what was her name, Señorita King, further embarrassment. But it seemed she had no appreciation of his motives.

The following morning Fernando's reservations had increased. He bitterly regretted the impulse he had had to give Eduardo an unexpected treat. It was giving Lucie the entirely false impression that he wished to see her again, and nothing could have been further from the truth. After showering and dressing and breakfasting in his suite at the Savoy, he had an almost overwhelming inclination to telephone the Castana house and make

8

some excuse for not taking the boy out that morning, but he could not bring himself to act so selfishly. Instead, he dressed in a navy denim suit with a belted jacket, combed his thick straight hair and decided it needed cutting, and took a taxi to Lorrimer Terrace before he had second thoughts.

A young maid admitted him to the now quiet house. Only the pervading aroma of stale cigarette smoke and a faint drift of perfume evidenced the party of the night before, and he waited impatiently in the morning room, eager to be gone.

A few minutes later the maid reappeared. 'Master Eduardo will be ready presently, sir,' she said. 'And Señora Castana suggests that you take lunch with her on your return.'

Fernando's mouth turned down at the corners, and the maid who was watching him thought what an attractive mouth it was. He was an attractive man altogether, without the somewhat swarthy case to his skin that Señor Castana himself had. He was tall, too, taller than the average Spaniard, though not so tall as to appear ungainly. His hair was dark, but not black, and his clothes fitted him closely, emphasizing the powerful length of his legs and the muscular expanse of his chest.

'You may inform Señora Castana after I have gone that I shall be unable to accept her invitation,' he stated quietly. 'I am not sure, but Eduardo and I may – take lunch out.'

The maid looked surprised, and Fernando conceded that perhaps he had spoken a little bluntly. But there was no other way to avoid difficulties. So long as Carlos was away on business, Lucie was a menace.

There was the sound of footsteps behind them in the hall and Fernando swung round as Eduardo came into the room followed closely by the young woman he knew as Señorita King. Inclining his head, he spoke to both of them: 'Good morning, Eduardo. Good morning, Miss King.'

Eduardo gave a little skip. At seven years of age, a trip to the zoo was an exciting experience. 'Are you ready to

9

go, *señor*?' he demanded eagerly.

Fernando smiled. 'I see you are,' he commented, still speaking English.

'Oh, yes. I have been waiting for you to come for hours!' declared Eduardo, with characteristic exaggeration.

Fernando shifted his attention to the young woman. This morning she was not wearing the nylon overall, but he suspected the neat grey skirt, the white shirt blouse and broad black belt signified some kind of uniform. Her hair, too, had been plaited and formed a coronet on top of her head. Although she was slim, she was not thin, and he could see the rounded swell of her breasts pressing against the material of her blouse. He looked away quickly, conscious of an unaccustomed quickening of his senses. It was not like him to notice such things, and he despised himself for doing so. The girl was nothing to him, and from the way she was looking at him he sensed she objected strongly to his appraisal.

'Well—' he began determinedly, forcing an enthusiasm he did not feel. 'Shall we go?'

They all moved out into the hall and the maid departed about her business. The girl secured the zip on Eduardo's anorak and stepped aside. But even as she did so a voice hailed them from above, a voice Fernando recognized only too well.

'Fernando! Oh, Fernando, you are still here! I am so glad I have caught you.'

Lucie was standing on the stairs, a flimsy negligée draped about her. The girl, Miss King, seemed embarrassed and would have left them, but Fernando found himself doing something he had never intended to do. He looked up at Lucie, but as he did so he spoke in an undertone to the girl: 'Get your coat, Miss King. You are coming with us.'

She stared at him as if he was mad, but Lucie was speaking again and Fernando had to move reluctantly towards the stairs.

'If you will wait a few minutes, Fernando,' she was saying, 'I will come with you. That is . . .' her lips curved provocatively, 'that is – if you do not mind.'

Fernando thrust his hands into the pockets of his jacket. 'Do you think it is your sort of outing, Lucie?' he inquired dryly. 'Er – you are aware that Miss King is accompanying us, are you not?'

Lucie's brows drew together. 'Miss King?'

'But of course.' Fernando was charming. He turned to look into the girl's indignant, but as yet impotent, face. 'Is that not so, Miss King?'

It was the moment of truth, the moment he dreaded. He was daring her to deny it. But to his relief she merely bent her head and said in muffled tones: 'Yes, of course, *señor*.'

Lucie looked almost as angry as she had done the night before, but she controlled herself by a supreme effort and said: 'In that case, there is no point, is there, *caro*?' She took a deep breath. 'Instead, I shall await your return with impatience. Did the maid tell you that I expect you to stay for lunch?'

Fernando sighed. 'She did. But I cannot.'

'Why not?' Lucie was angry again.

'It is not possible, Lucie. The zoo is a large place. I do not expect to be back before – well – four o'clock.'

'Four o'clock!' Lucie was furious. She gathered the negligée closer about her, apparently uncaring of the fact of its transparency. 'Very well, then. You will dine with us, *si*?'

Fernando hesitated. To issue a firm refusal could continue this discussion interminably. With a faint shrug, he said: 'Perhaps, Lucie, perhaps.' He forced a smile. 'We must be going. I have a taxi waiting.'

Lucie's jaw was taut. 'Until dinner, then.'

Fernando gave her a small bow. 'Until later,' he agreed, non-committally.

Miss King put on a grey coat to match her skirt and accompanied him out to the cab. They all climbed in and not until Eduardo was staring in an engrossed manner out of the window did she say: 'I should be glad if you would never place me in such an awkward position again, *señor*! The invitation you issued was for Eduardo alone, and you know it!'

Fernando lay back in his seat, half turned towards her, watching her intently. Her voice was low and angry, but it had a husky intonation which he found pleasing. When she was angry, as now, she was disturbingly feminine, and not even the plain, even ugly, uniform could disguise that. He wondered what she would look like in casual clothes? He wondered what her name was. How old she was.

Realizing she was waiting for him to make some comment, he said: 'All right. It was – initially. However, I thought that perhaps you might enjoy the outing—'

'I don't believe you!' She was abrupt.

'Oh, really?' Fernando didn't altogether care for her manner. 'Is not that a rather insolent remark?'

She sighed. 'I'm not blind, *señor*. Nor am I a fool.'

'I never imagined you were.'

'Nevertheless, that was not the reason you insisted on my company, and I'd be grateful if in future you'd refrain from using me to extricate yourself from situations which have grown too hot for you!'

'Why, you—' He bit off an epithet, conscious that for the first time in his life he had the urge to strike a woman. He stared at her angrily. No one had ever spoken to him in such a manner, would ever *dare* to do so! He was enraged, not least because although in one way she was speaking the truth, his own involvement was such an innocent one. 'Do you realize I could put you out of this cab here and now, drive back to Señora Castana, and have you dismissed at once!'

She shook her head. 'That's entirely up to you, of course.'

'Don't you care?' He was astounded.

She hesitated. 'Well, I shouldn't like to lose my job for incompetence, but this is rather different, isn't it?'

Fernando chewed his lower lip. He had never met anyone quite like her before, and as his anger dispersed almost as quickly as it had come he found himself in the ignominious position of wanting to explain his motivations.

Frowning, he said: 'I see no reason why I should justify my actions to you, but I can assure you that while there might be some truth in your suggestion that I invited you to evade—' He glanced at Eduardo rather significantly. 'Well – to evade certain people, the situation is by no means too – *hot* – for me!'

She pressed her lips together and he had the disturbing suspicion that she was trying not to smile, a suspicion which was increased when she looked up at him.

'You're laughing at me!' he accused irritably.

'No, I'm not.' She made a helpless gesture. 'Besides, what you choose to do with your time is no concern of mine except where it impinges on mine.'

'*Madre mia*, I know it's not!' he snapped shortly, angry now that he had tried to explain. 'If you would rather not accompany us then I shall direct the driver to take you back again,' he added, in stiff tones.

She looked at him then and he saw that her eyes were a curious shade of deep violet, African violet, dark and beautiful. 'I didn't actually say that I didn't want to accompany you,' she said carefully. 'Only that I didn't wish to be involved in – in schemes.'

'My schemes?'

'If you like.'

'You still believe—' He broke off. 'I give you my word. Lucie – that is – your employer and I are friends, that is all.'

Her lids fell to hide her expression. 'If you say so, *señor*.'

Fernando controlled an almost irresistible desire to shake her. Was she deliberately goading him? Or was the image of Lucie in her negligée so firmly imprinted upon her mind as to negate anything he might say? He couldn't be sure. He didn't even know why he felt bound to try and explain.

Changing his tack, he inclined his head and said: 'Very well, Miss King. I suggest we forget the unfortunate beginning and try and enjoy the day.' He frowned. 'We have not even been introduced. Fernando Cuevas, at your service, *señorita*.'

13

It was beholden upon her to make some similar statement, but she was obviously reluctant. He wondered why. His experience of women had taught him that he was invariably regarded in a favourable light, and while he did not normally make any effort to exert the charm which came so naturally to him, it was galling to realize that to this young woman he represented something else.

At last she said: 'My name is Susannah, *señor*, Susannah King.'

'Susannah.' He repeated the word reflectively. It suited her. It was a wholly feminine appellation.

Eduardo turned from the window at that moment, gesticulating excitedly. '*Señorita, señorita*, is that St. Paul's *catedral*? You said you would take me there one day, *señorita*. Will you? Will you?'

Susannah leant forward and then smiled. 'Oh, no, Eduardo, that's not St. Paul's. That's just a church. St. Paul's is bigger, much bigger.'

'Perhaps you would permit me to escort you both there another day,' suggested Fernando. 'Perhaps tomorrow?'

As soon as the words were uttered he wondered why he had said them. He had been reluctant to come out this morning. What was he thinking of – suggesting yet another visit to the Castana house?

Susannah King was looking at him strangely too. Perhaps she suspected some ulterior motive for his suggestion. He cursed himself for putting himself in such an ambiguous situation.

'That's very kind of you, *señor*,' she was saying now, 'but Eduardo has lessons tomorrow.'

Eduardo's face dropped and the relief Fernando should have felt did not materialize. Instead, he found himself saying: 'You give Eduardo these lessons, Miss King?'

'Yes.'

'You are then the boy's – governess?'

'That's right,' she nodded.

'But I do not understand. Yesterday evening you were acting as nursemaid.'

She sighed. 'Señora Castana has no nursemaid for

Eduardo. She says she likes to look after him herself. When she cannot, I – I cope.'

Fernando found this knowledge not to his liking. Back home in Spain one employed a governess to teach, a nursemaid to care for the child's welfare. Lucie knew this as well as he did. Surely they were not so short of financial assets that they could not afford both. But no. The Castanas were a wealthy family. It was much more likely, though not so palatable, that so long as Miss King was prepared to accommodate them they preferred to save a second salary.

They were driving now beside the green stretches of Regent's Park, and Fernando leant forward and signified to the driver that they would walk the rest of the way. Susannah and the boy climbed out, Fernando paid their fare, and the cab rolled away.

It was a cool but pleasant morning in early April. Spring was in the air and the park was colourful with tulips and daffodils and narcissi. Even at this time of day there were plenty of people about, nannies with their charges, young mothers with prams, dogs and their owners enjoying the unexpectedly warm sunshine. They walked along the path towards the zoological gardens and conversation between them lapsed. Only Eduardo seemed unaware of the fact, exclaiming every now and then when a dog ran near to them or a child with a particularly interesting toy attracted his attention.

Zoos had never appealed to Fernando. The idea of a collection of wild animals being confined in small spaces for the public to come and stare at seemed to him a rather cruel and degrading arrangement. But when he remarked upon this to Susannah King he found that she had very definite ideas of her own upon the subject.

'Most of these animals were born in captivity,' she exclaimed. 'They'd be no more at home in the wild than – than say, you would be, cast away on some desert island, remote from all the sophisticated accoutrements to civilized society you've grown used to.'

Fernando smiled. 'And how do you know how I would react to such circumstances?' he commented with a trace of irony. 'I might find such a situation intriguing – depending, of course, on my companion.'

He saw the rose colour flood her cheeks. He was surprised at how easily he could embarrass her. So self-confident in some ways, in others she was extremely vulnerable, and the knowledge troubled him. He found himself wondering about her background, whether she had any home life, whether her parents were still alive – and then stopped himself. This would not do. After today, he would probably never see her again, which was just as well. He was becoming far too interested in her. He was leaving England at the end of the week. He was returning to his home in Spain – to his own family.

He noticed that after that she did not speak to him directly for some time, but concentrated on Eduardo, pointing out different species, explaining their various eating habits. Fernando was quite content to stroll along behind, answering Eduardo's questions only when they were addressed to him.

It was after one o'clock when Susannah seemed to become aware of the lateness of the hour, and casting a doubtful look in Fernando's direction said: 'I think Eduardo ought to have a drink and something to eat, *señor*. Could we go to the café and have a sandwich?'

Fernando hesitated. The café, within sight and sound, not to mention smell, of the animals did not appeal to him. 'I suggest we leave the gardens and find a restaurant, *señorita*. Eduardo has seen almost everything, has he not? Perhaps this afternoon we might do something else, *si*?'

'*Que*?' Eduardo stared at them both excitedly. '*Que le parece, señorita*,' he appealed. '*Tengo mucha hombre!*'

'Speak English, Eduardo,' reproved Susannah automatically, and then gave a small shrug of her shoulders. 'I don't know what to say, *señor*.'

Fernando cupped her elbow with his hand. 'Then I suggest you leave everything to me,' he remarked quietly. 'Eduardo is hungry. Were he and I alone, we would most certainly dine at a restaurant of my choosing. Your company simply makes that a more attractive proposition.'

Susannah drew herself away from him quickly, and he could see she was embarrassed again. For himself he was conscious of a distinct feeling of exhilaration in his stomach brought about by the trembling he had felt in that instant before she drew herself away.

They went to a Spanish restaurant in a mews off Oxford Street. It was a place Fernando frequented regularly on his visits to London, and he was recognized at once. The service was efficient, but unobtrusive, and he noticed that Susannah seemed to enjoy the onion soup, the chicken and rice, and the fruit-filled icecream which they ate as a dessert. They had a rosé wine with the meal, and even Eduardo drank his with enjoyment. Afterwards, the waiter brought coffee, and a liqueur for Fernando which Susannah had declined. Eduardo was excused and wandered off to examine an enormous aquarium filled with tropical fish which was an integral part of the wall near the entrance to the restaurant, and Fernando asked whether Susannah would mind if he lit a cheroot.

She shook her head. He could see that she was nervous and endeavoured to put her at her ease, talking about Spain in general terms, discussing the wine-growing industry of which his family had been members for generations.

'I know very little about wines,' she admitted, cradling her coffee cup between her fingers. 'They're not considered a natural accompaniment to a meal here – at least, not where I come from.'

'Where do you come from, Miss King?' Fernando questioned, unable to prevent himself from doing so.

She put down her cup. 'I was born in Yorkshire, actually. That's in the north of England. But when I had completed my training I came south to work.'

He drew deeply on his cheroot, exhaling into the air above her head. 'Your parents still live in Yorkshire?' he suggested.

'No. My parents are dead.' She sighed. 'Actually, I never knew who my parents were. I lived in an orphanage until I was sixteen years old – a children's home is

17

how they like to describe it.'

'You sound – bitter.'

'Oh, no, no.' She shook her head. 'I'm not bitter. They were very good to me, actually. I just don't think it's fair that women should have babies and then – abandon them. If I had a child, I'd want to care for it myself.' She flushed. 'Where is Eduardo?'

'Eduardo is quite happy watching the fish,' replied Fernando, impatient at the interruption. 'Go on. I'm interested.'

'There's nothing more to tell.'

'You've worked for the Castanas ever since you came to London?' He was surprised.

'No. No, not all the time. I've been here four years. I worked for an American family to begin with, but they divorced and I didn't want to go and live in the States, so I joined the Castanas six months ago.'

'I see,' he nodded. He had the feeling that Lucie Castana would not keep her staff very long. He dropped ash into the tray in the centre of the table and then said: 'Don't you want to get married? Have children – as you said.'

Susannah coloured again. 'Not for expediency, if that's what you mean, *señor*,' she stated stiffly, and he cursed himself for putting her on the offensive again. 'Don't you think it's time we were leaving.'

Fernando heaved a sigh. He could have gone on talking to her for a long time. There were many more things he would like to know about her, and this in itself was unusual for him. Women had always seemed vapidly transparent creatures, intent solely on finding a man and capturing him. Marriage was a convenience, for both sexes, and anything beyond that was purely a sexual necessity. He had never particularly cared for talking to a woman before, and he resented having to share her attention with the boy.

Outside the restaurant Eduardo had a stream of suggestions as to where they should spend the remainder of the afternoon, but Susannah was not disposed to listen to them. 'It's already getting on for three o'clock,' she declared. 'I'm sure we've taken up enough of Señor Cuevas' time already.'

Fernando thrust his hands into the pockets of his jacket. He wanted to detain her, and it would not be difficult with Eduardo beginning to sulk at having his afternoon cut short, but common sense warned him that he had gone far enough.

'I think perhaps Miss King is right, Eduardo,' he stated, looking up and down the street rather impatiently. 'Besides, you will want to go back and tell your mother what you have seen, will you not?'

Eduardo pouted. 'You said we would go somewhere else,' he accused, and Fernando felt a sense of contrition. He was letting the boy down simply because it was easier for him that way, and that wasn't altogether kind.

'Another day,' he conceded at last. 'If Miss King will permit you to miss lessons.'

Susannah gave a faint smile. 'Thank you very much for escorting us, *señor*, and for that most delicious lunch.'

'*No tanto*. It was nothing.' Fernando could hear the stiffness in his voice, but her attempted dismissal irritated him. It was one thing for him to decide that they must part and quite another for her to take it upon herself to dismiss him. 'I will accompany you back to the house, naturally.'

Susannah gave him a startled look. 'That's not necessary. That is—' She paused, and he could almost read her thoughts. 'Of course you are at liberty to come with us if you wish.'

'As far as the door at least,' he conceded sardonically, and was gratified to see that he had disconcerted her again.

But when the cab halted outside the Castana house in Lorrimer Terrace and Eduardo bounded out, intent on regaling everyone with his experiences, Fernando stayed Susannah with a hand on her arm. 'One moment, *señorita*,' he said in a low voice, aware of the troubled anxiety in her eyes.

'Yes, *señor*?'

She sounded cool while he could feel heated blood in

his veins. He drew a deep breath. 'I wish you to have dinner with me tomorrow evening, Miss King.'

Her eyes fell before his, looking at his lean brown hand on the grey material of her sleeve. 'I'm afraid I can't, *señor*,' she refused politely.

Anger erupted. '*Por dios*, why not?'

She tried to draw away. 'I don't think it's a very good idea, *señor*. I – I don't have a lot of free time in the evenings in any case.'

'I think you are making excuses, Miss King. Why? Do you not trust me? I assure you, my motives are quite innocent. I enjoy talking with you, that is all.'

Susannah looked after Eduardo. 'I must go, *señor*. Eduardo will tell his mother we are here. It would not do for her to find me here, with you, would it?'

An ironic smile touched his lips. 'It is not of the slightest consequence to me whether or not Lucie finds us together.' His eyes darkened. 'Please – you will have dinner with me tomorrow evening, *si*?'

When he was disturbed his accent thickened, and he could hear it thickening now as he appealed to her. Why was it so important that she should accept his invitation?

She looked at him in an anxious fashion and then made a helpless little gesture. 'I don't know—' she began awkwardly.

'At eight,' he insisted, pressing his advantage. 'Walk to the end of the terrace and I will be waiting.'

'*Señor*—' she started, when Fernando saw Lucie appear in the doorway and look rather impatiently towards the cab.

He withdrew his hand from Susannah's arm, and said: 'Here is your employer now. Shall we get out to greet her?'

Susannah stepped awkwardly out of the cab and almost fell as she ricked her ankle on the kerb. But Lucie took not the slightest notice of her. Her eyes were intent on Fernando, and asking the cab-driver to wait, he too climbed out.

'You're early,' she exclaimed, with a little dismissing

nod in Susannah's direction. 'Come along in. We can have some tea.'

'*Gracias, no*, Lucie.' Fernando lapsed back into his own language. 'I must go. I have an appointment with the importers at five o'clock.'

Lucie's lips drew in. 'You did not say that this morning, Fernando. I cancelled an afternoon engagement to be here on your return.'

'I am sorry.' He gave an apologetic smile.

Lucie held up her head. He could see she was warring with herself whether or not to mention the tentative dinner engagement also, but before she could come to a decision he bade her a brief *Adios* and climbed back into the cab. He could see the angry frustration in her face as he drove away and he hoped she would not wreak that frustration on Susannah King.

CHAPTER TWO

Susannah was supervising Eduardo's tea in the nursery when Lucie Castana came to find her. She could tell at once that Lucie was in a fine temper, and she hoped she would not start an argument here in front of the boy. He saw enough of that sort of thing between his father and mother and while Señor Castana was away Susannah had hoped to avoid any unpleasantness. However, her hopes were short-lived. Lucie was in no mood to prevaricate and came straight to the point.

'Exactly what did you mean by going off for the day like that without asking my permission, *señorita*?' she snapped angrily.

Eduardo looked up from his boiled egg in surprise. 'Don Fernando asked Señorita King to come with us,' he declared, in his boyish treble.

'Keep out of this, Eduardo!' Lucie ignored him. 'Well, *señorita*? I am waiting for your explanation.'

Susannah moved away from the tea table. 'I saw no objection to my joining Eduardo and – and Don Fernando, *señora*,' she replied carefully. 'There is nothing for me to do here when Eduardo is out.'

'I might have had other ideas on the subject, *señorita*. It is true, you are employed for Eduardo's sake, but I expect some consideration from you. I will not have you inviting yourself on every expedition that Eduardo makes simply because there is nothing for you to do here!'

'It wasn't like that, *señora*—' Susannah was indignant.

'Do not answer me back, *señorita*! If I say it was like that, then it was like that, do you understand?' Lucie's dark eyes flashed maliciously. 'I did not realize you were so desperate for male companionship. Of course, while Carlos is away I've no doubt you miss his support—'

'How dare you?' Susannah was trembling with anger. 'How – how dare you? Exactly what are you implying,

22

señora?'

Now it was Lucie's turn to look discomfited. For a moment she had allowed her own feelings of jealousy and frustration to get the better of her, but now she was regretting speaking so bluntly. In the eighteen months they had lived in England she had employed a total of five different governesses for Eduardo, and all except Susannah had left within three months of their employment. Only Susannah had borne the arduous duties pressed upon her without complaint, and Lucie knew that if Carlos came home to find that she, too, had given in her notice, he would be furious.

Taking a deep breath, she put out an apologetic hand and said: 'I am sorry, *señorita*. Naturally, I am not implying anything.' She forced a faint smile. 'I – I have a headache, and I was looking forward to taking tea with Don Fernando. Unfortunately he has a business engagement, and I am afraid I allowed my disappointment to erupt into an unjustified anger against you.'

Susannah linked her fingers tightly together. 'If you have any cause for complaint about my behaviour—'

Lucie shook her head impatiently. 'No, no. Have I not just said I am sorry?' She half turned. 'I gather from Eduardo that you have had an enjoyable day.'

Susannah quelled the urge to tell Lucie Castana exactly what she thought of her as she caught sight of Eduardo's concerned face. He was not ignorant of what had so nearly occurred, and there was appeal as well as anxiety in his eyes.

'We had a – very enjoyable day, *señora*,' she conceded at last, in expressionless tones.

Lucie studied her profile for a few moments and then walked towards the door. 'So – we will forget this unpleasantness, *si*?' she requested, unable to leave without gaining some sort of assurance from the girl.

Susannah made an indifferent movement of her shoulders. 'Very well, *señora*,' she agreed without enthusiasm, and Lucie had to be content with that.

Eduardo went to bed at seven o'clock and usually after this Susannah's time was her own. Occasionally, when the Castanas were having a party, they asked her to remain in her rooms in case the boy needed her, but these occasions were not frequent.

Susannah herself did not go out a lot. She liked plays and sometimes a film, and if she was invited to a concert she enjoyed that very much, but she had no regular routine. Her friends were mostly girls from the training college she had attended, and although one or two of them were now married and introduced her to lots of suitable young men, she had no steady boy-friend. She was in no hurry to get married. Her background had not endeared the opposite sex to her, knowing as she did that her mother had been abandoned by her father when he found that she was pregnant. Or at least, that was her interpretation of her mother's incapacity to care for her herself.

That evening, Susannah changed out of her formal skirt and blouse, donned an old pair of jeans and a chunky sweater, and settled down with the novel she had been reading for the past few evenings. It was a saga of family life in Cornwall at the turn of the century and up until now had inspired her interest. But this evening she found it hard to concentrate on imaginary characters when her mind kept wandering back over the real events of the day. She had no intention of accepting Fernando Cuevas's invitation to dinner. She had been employed as a governess long enough to know that getting involved with either a member of the family or with a friend of a member of that family was simply asking for trouble. When she had worked for the American family, the Taylors, she had had plenty of opportunities, but she had learned her lesson well. Now she knew better than to cultivate relationships which in her position could only cause difficulties.

All the same, that did not stop her from thinking about him. He was the most attractive man she had ever met and although he did not possess the even good looks people referred to as handsome there was something disturbingly magnetic about deep-set, heavy-lidded eyes, a lean intelligent face, and smooth dark hair that appeared to need none of the oily hairdressing so loved by other

Latin men she had met. She wondered how old he was – possibly between thirty-five and forty, but she couldn't be sure. He didn't look old, but the experience in his eyes betrayed an awareness not evident in the eyes of a younger man. She wondered why he had asked her to dine with him. What possible motive could he have? She didn't believe his statement about enjoying talking to her, and she was not conceited enough to imagine that he might be attracted by her appearance. It would have been quite an experience, she acknowledged truthfully, but experiences sometimes required a payment she was not prepared to give.

The following day it crossed her mind that she really ought to ask Señora Castana for Señor Cuevas' telephone number while he was here in London and ring and explain that she would not be meeting him that evening. But discretion got the better of valour. To bring up such a thing would only create more trouble, and she decided that if he did come to meet her and she did not turn up that would be that.

But as the day drew towards evening she had second thoughts. What if, when she did not go to meet him, he came to the house? What would she do then? What could she do? And how incensed Lucie Castana would be!

She put Eduardo to bed at seven o'clock as usual, said good night, and went to her own rooms. Señor Castana was due home tomorrow and Señora Castana had told her that she intended having an early night. There was no reason why she should not slip out of the house, meet Señor Cuevas and explain, and be back indoors again before anyone noticed her absence.

The decision made, she changed out of her uniform into a pair of rather shabby red velvet pants and a cream ribbed sweater, leaving her hair in the coronet of plaits she had worn all day. At five minutes to eight she left the house, not bothering with a coat but throwing a thigh-length cream cardigan about her shoulders.

It was a mild evening and the birds were still making a loud noise in the small park across the way. There were few people about. This small terrace of elegant town houses was occupied by a section of the community to whom walking was something one only did on the golf course, so she met no one she knew as she hurried towards the corner. There was no sign of Fernando Cuevas and unreasonably her heart sank. What did it matter? she asked herself impatiently. If he didn't turn up, all the better. It would save her having to go into unnecessary explanations.

Reaching the end of the street, she looked up and down the wider thoroughfare beyond, but there was no one around who looked the slightest bit like the lean dark Spaniard she had come to meet. She sighed and consulted the broad masculine watch on her slim wrist. It was only just eight o'clock. He might conceivably be late. Traffic in London at this hour of the evening was notoriously unreliable, and it was quite easy to get trapped in a jam.

She drew her cardigan closer about her, shifting her weight from one foot to the other. She might as well wait a few minutes. If only to satisfy herself that she had been wasting her time.

'Good evening, Miss King!'

The quiet words spoken somewhere near her ear startled her almost out of her wits and she swung round on her heels staring in amazement at the man who was standing just behind her. He was quite close and she could smell a faint aroma of an after-shaving lotion. He was casually dressed in a tawny-coloured lounge suit and a roll-collared silk shirt that clung to the contours of his chest as he moved. His eyes dropped the length of her body in a swift appraising motion and then returned to her face again as he smiled approvingly.

'I am glad you have dressed informally,' he said. 'I was afraid you might take my invitation to mean a dinner jacket affair.'

Susannah gathered herself. 'No, no, you don't understand, *señor*. I – I didn't come to meet you, at least – not to go out with you.'

His eyes narrowed. 'What is that supposed to mean, *señorita*?'

Susannah folded the sleeves of her cardigan around her

arms. I can't dine with you, *señor*. I'm sorry. I tried to make it plain yesterday afternoon, but Señora Castana interrupted me, and—'

'*Basta!*' He cut her off with an impatient ejaculation. 'Why can you not dine with me? You are here. You are ready. Where is the difficulty?'

Susannah gasped, 'I'm not ready. Not like this!'

'You look perfectly satisfactory to me.' He shook his head. 'Why did you come to meet me if you did not wish to dine with me?'

Susannah shrugged. 'I – I was afraid you might come to the house. I didn't want to cause any more – upset.'

'With whom? Señora Castana?'

'Does it matter?' She moved a little away from him. 'I'm very flattered, of course, but I don't accept invitations from friends of my employers.'

Fernando Cuevas put out a hand and caught her upper arm preventing her further progress, his fingers hard and compelling. 'Why not? Do your employers forbid it? Do they subject you to a very subtle form of moral blackmail?'

Susannah shook her head, looking down at his hand on her arm. 'It doesn't do to mix business with pleasure,' she replied. Then she looked up. 'I'd have thought you would have known that, *señor*.'

He smiled, the kind of smile that caused her heart to quicken its beat rather dramatically. 'Please,' he said appealingly. 'Would you disappoint a lonely man? A stranger to your country? I promise not to compromise you in any way.' He glanced over his shoulder. 'Come. I have a car this evening – I hired it specially for the occasion. I do not care for taxi drivers to listen to all my conversations with you.'

Susannah's resolve was weakening by the second. Her head was swimming, and she wondered if he could feel the throbbing rate of her pulses through his fingers gripping her arm. She thought it was entirely possible. There was a certainty of purpose about him now which was not completely due to his own self-confidence. Slowly but surely he was drawing her with him, off the pavement and on to the road and across to where a gold-coloured Ford Granada was parked, the reason why she had not observed him earlier.

'You see,' he said, unlocking the door with his key. 'Is this not a most attractive vehicle I have chosen for us?'

Susannah looked into his face, so disturbingly close to her own. 'Where are you taking me?'

'Get in and you will find out,' he advised quietly.

She hesitated for a moment and then with a resigned shrug she allowed him to assist her into the car and close the door behind her. He walked round the bonnet and slid in beside her, giving her a slight smile as he did so, and she thought with a sense of self-betrayal that for once she was allowing a man to call the tune.

Fernando said nothing as he threaded his way expertly through the busy traffic and on to the Hammersmith flyover. She had expected him to be uncertain of his way about London, but it seemed obvious that he was used to driving through its maze of one-way streets and box junctions. Susannah sat in the comfortable leather seat, separated from him by the console fixture of the gear lever, and wondered exactly where they were going.

As the traffic thinned, he had more time to look about him, and settling himself more comfortably in his seat, he said: 'How old are you, Miss King?'

Susannah was taken aback. 'That's a very pointed question, isn't it?'

'Hmm. I suppose it is. Are you going to tell me?' He looked at her out of the corners of his eyes, and she found herself becoming warm under his gaze.

'As a matter of fact I'm twenty-four,' she declared shortly. 'How old are you?'

He chuckled. 'Much older than that, Miss King.'

'That's not an answer,' she exclaimed indignantly.

'How old do you think I am?'

She hesitated. 'I'm not sure. Thirty-five, thirty-six?'

'You're too kind.' His expression was wry. 'I am forty, Miss King. Almost old enough to be your father, *si*?'

She bent her head. 'Why did you want to know how old I was?'

He shrugged, resting his arm on the ledge of his window. 'I had the distinct suspicion that you were much younger than twenty-four. Were it not for that ridiculous hairstyle, I would say you were twenty at most.'

'Ridiculous hairstyle!' she echoed, putting a hand to her head. 'What's ridiculous about it?'

He cast her a sardonic glance. 'You look like a small girl trying to look like an adult. I liked it better in the elastic bands, untidy though it was.'

Susannah caught her breath. 'I don't think you should make personal comments about my appearance, *señor*.'

'No. I agree, I should not. But you did ask me, and I was merely being truthful.' He slowed behind a lumbering wagon. 'And as I am so much older than you are, perhaps it would not be too presumptuous of me to suggest that I might call you Susannah, *si*?'

She clasped her hands tightly together in her lap. 'Do I have any choice?'

'You make me sound very rude. I'm sorry.'

She sighed. 'I didn't mean to do so. Of course you may call me Susannah if you wish.'

His lean brown fingers slid round the wheel. 'So. As that is disposed of, I suggest we talk about something else. For example – do you like shellfish?'

'Shellfish, *señor*?' She sounded as perplexed as she felt.

'*Si*. Is that not how you say it – lobster, crab, that kind of thing?'

'Oh, I see. Shellfish.' She nodded apologetically. 'Yes, I like it.'

'That is good. The place where we are to dine serves the most delicious lobster you have ever tasted. It is cooked in a sauce of cream and white wine, and melts in the mouth. You must try it.'

Susannah managed a smile, but in truth she was wondering whether she would be able to eat anything at all. His presence unnerved her. She felt the restraint between them like a tangible thing. And yet there was no reason for it.

To her surprise, their destination was a rather exclusive golf club, overlooking the Thames near Kingston. Although on this Wednesday evening there appeared to be no rule about formality, many of the diners were wearing dinner jackets, or lounge suits with bow ties, and as their female counterparts all looked elegant and soignée to Susannah's uneasy eyes, she felt terribly self-conscious in her old velvet pants and cream sweater.

It was better once they were seated at table and Fernando was studying the wine list. What small interest their arrival had aroused had mostly been concentrated on him, but now that he was patently ignoring it the conversation around them resumed its normal level.

The meal was as delicious as he had said it would be, and under his surveillance she agreed to try the lobster. A certain amount of good wine loosened her reserve and while they ate she talked quite happily about her work, relating one or two amusing anecdotes she had collected over the years. He was a good listener. He lay back in his seat watching her closely, and it was not until they reached the coffee stage that she realized she still knew absolutely nothing about him, other than that he was a friend of the Castanas. He wore three rings, two very broad silver ones and a meshed gold one, but none of them occupied the third finger of his left hand. Even so, he could be married for all she knew. And she had no idea how to bring the conversation round to his personal affairs.

They left the restaurant at about ten o'clock and walked back to the gold Granada. It was parked beneath a willow tree that dipped its branches towards the river. It was cooler now than it had been when they left London a couple of hours ago, and Susannah shivered.

'You are cold,' he said at once, unlocking her door. 'Do get in. I should not like you to catch a chill, Susannah.'

She climbed inside obediently and watched him through the rear-view mirror as he walked round the back of the car to reach his door. He levered himself in beside her, checked that she was comfortable, and then reversed smoothly out of the parking area.

It seemed no time at all before they were running through the suburbs, dark now with street lamps casting pools of light on the pavements. He drove through the mass of side streets to reach Lorrimer Terrace, and brought the big car to a halt only a few feet from the door of the Castana house.

Susannah glanced doubtfully up at the windows, wondering whether their return had been observed. It was unlikely. Lucie Castana slept at the back of the building and the sound of a car drawing up in the street outside was a common enough occurrence for it not to attract any especial interest.

She suddenly realized that she was making no attempt to get out of the car and turning to Fernando Cuevas, she said: 'Thank you very much, *señor*. I have enjoyed myself.'

The dark Spaniard gave her a slight smile, his fingers tapping somewhat impatiently on the wheel. 'That is good,' he replied. 'So have I. Good night, Susannah.'

'Good night, *señor*.'

With a vague feeling of reluctance, she climbed out of the car and he leant across to close her door behind her, giving her a casual salute before driving away. She entered the house with a distinctly hollow emptiness inside that owed nothing to her physical condition. She didn't know what she had expected. She should have felt relieved that he had made no attempt to ask to see her again. But she didn't. Instead, she felt emotionally drained, deflated, and totally out of humour with herself for feeling so.

The following day life resumed its normal pattern. Eduardo had lessons in the morning and in the afternoon they walked to the common so that he could run off some of the energy he had in such abundance. Susannah usually enjoyed these outings. She liked running about after the ball and seeing Eduardo's pale face flushed with healthy colour as he forgot his anxieties in the pure delight of physical exertion.

But today, Susannah found it hard to relax. She was

constantly searching for a gold Granada among the cars that they passed and every dark man they encountered aroused a momentary flutter of excitement which was just as quickly doused. She didn't know why she should imagine that Fernando Cuevas might want to see her again. His parting of the night before had been humiliatingly brief. And yet she couldn't deny the surge of anticipation she was feeling.

However, neither a gold Granada nor any dark Spaniard appeared and she returned to the house for afternoon tea somewhat dejectedly. Señor Castana had returned in their absence and when Eduardo saw his father waiting for him in the hall he gave an excited squeal and ran towards him eagerly. Susannah greeted her employer politely and then left the family together, asking the young maid to bring her tea to her sitting-room.

The next morning Señor Castana sent for Susannah while she was giving Eduardo his lessons. Leaving the boy writing out an English exercise in his laborious fashion she went downstairs to the study wondering whether Señora Castana had found some cause for complaint in spite of what she had said.

Carlos Castana was a stocky man of average height, with a thin moustache. He was handsome in a swarthy, Latin sort of way, but Susannah liked him because he had such a pleasant personality. He always tried to be fair in his dealings with the staff, and they all thought he put up with his wife's moods and tempers very patiently. Now he admitted Susannah to his study, rather thoughtfully she thought, and indicated that she should take a seat. Susannah sat, waiting apprehensively for him to begin. Of course, he might just want a report on Eduardo's progress, but in the past he had always come to the schoolroom for that.

He walked behind his desk and sat down facing her. 'First of all, Miss King, I want to say how pleased we are with Eduardo's development.'

Susannah folded her hands in her lap. 'Thank you, *señor.*'

He shook his head. 'No, I am thanking you, Miss King. You have settled down with us very well – better than I had dared to hope.' He paused. 'You may know that in the past my wife has had some difficulties in keeping staff, but I'm glad to say that you appear to have fitted in with us excellently.'

'Thank you, *señor*.'

Susannah was intrigued. She wondered what all this was leading up to. If Señor Castana hadn't brought her here to discipline her, what did he want?

He went on, choosing his words carefully. 'As you are aware, I have been abroad for several days. I went to the continent on business. There was a directors' meeting. My company is planning to expand.'

Susannah nodded. She didn't quite know why he was telling her this. The affairs of his company were nothing to do with her, unless it was a roundabout way of telling her that he intended giving her a rise.

He reached for a cigar from the box on his desk, and lit it before going on. Then, when it was glowing warmly, giving off an aroma of Havana tobacco, he said: 'The company is planning to open a branch in New York, Miss King. I have been invited to run that branch.'

Now she understood. He was explaining the circumstances to her because if he took this appointment, if he moved to New York, he would expect his family to move too, and that included Susannah herself as Eduardo's governess.

'I see,' she said inadequately.

'You understand why I am telling you this, do you not, Miss King? Naturally I shall be accepting this appointment and moving to New York. I intend to take a house there as I have done here for the past eighteen months. I want you to come with us.'

Susannah nodded. 'Yes.'

'You'll come?' He rose to his feet, resting his palms on the desk and leaning towards her.

'I don't know, *señor*. I – I should have to think about it.'

Señor Castana nodded. 'I understand that. I have told you at once because I remember at the time you came for an interview you mentioned that you were leaving your previous post because you did not wish to move to the United States. May I hope that you have changed your ideas since then?'

Susannah shrugged her shoulders. 'I don't know, *señor*. I – if it had been France – or Spain!' She hesitated. 'New York is such a long way away.'

'But you have no family in England, Miss King. You told me so yourself.'

'No,' she admitted. 'But my friends are here.'

'You will make new friends!' He spread a hand in a very continental gesture. 'You are a very attractive young woman, Miss King. Forgive me, but one cannot help but notice such things. I have seen the way men look at you . . . I do not think you would find it too difficult to find companionship.'

Susannah's cheeks were flushed. 'Well – thank you, *señor*. But really, I – I must have time to think it over.'

'Of course, of course. I will not rush you. I do not suppose we will be leaving England for several months yet. But I would hope you would decide soon. I want an English governess for Eduardo, and if you are not coming with us . . .'

'I quite understand, *señor*.' Susannah rose now. 'And – and thank you for your confidence in me.'

Señor Castana made some deprecatory comment before showing her out, but after the study door was closed, Susannah stood for several minutes in the hall thinking over what had been said before returning to the schoolroom. She was still standing there when the maid came down the stairs.

'Oh, there you are, Miss King,' she exclaimed. 'I've been up to the schoolroom looking for you. There's a letter been delivered for you.'

'A letter? For me?' Susannah forced herself to remain calm. 'Where – where is it?'

'It's here, miss.' The maid drew an envelope out of the

pocket of her apron. 'Delivered by hand, it was. Do you know who it's from?'

Susannah took the envelope from the maid's inquisitive hands, turning it over with trembling fingers. It was parchment-stiff, the quality evident, and there was a monogram on the flap. Making no attempt to open it, she stared at the scrawling handwriting and her heart skipped a beat. It had to be from him, it just had to.

Aware that the young maid was watching her eagerly, waiting for her to open it, she went towards the stairs and ran up them lightly. 'Thank you,' she called over her shoulder, and guessed that her concealment of the letter's contents would become the topic of much gossip and speculation in the kitchen. But she couldn't bear to open it in front of anyone else.

She went to the schoolroom first and checked that Eduardo was still busy, then she went to her own suite of rooms. Once inside she tore open the envelope and drew out the sheet of thick paper it contained. It was a letter, and an urgent glance at the signature at the end assured her of its writer's identity.

Dear Susannah, she read,

As you do not wish me to come to the house and as I cannot telephone without revealing my identity, I am forced to use this method of contacting you. I would like to see you again. I am expected to return to Spain on Sunday and therefore I would hope that we might dine together this evening or tomorrow evening. I realize that this is very short notice, that you may have some previous engagement, but I very much want to see you again, Susannah, and I shall wait in anticipation of your reply. You may reach me at the hotel at the head of this page.

Yours, Fernando Cuevas.

She re-read the letter twice, sitting on the edge of her armchair, conscious of a rising sense of exhilaration out of all proportion to the situation. But she couldn't help it.

To know that she was going to see him again filled her with excited expectation.

Putting the letter away carefully in her handbag, she returned to the schoolroom. As soon as she could she would ask Señor Castana whether she had any objections to her going out that evening. Now that Señor Castana was home surely no one would mind. Then she would telephone Fernando Cuevas's hotel while she and Eduardo were out walking this afternoon.

To her delight, Lucie Castana came to the schoolroom some fifteen minutes later and after speaking to Eduardo and complimenting him upon his painstaking work, she said: 'Señorita, my husband and I will be dining out this evening.' She didn't seem to notice Susannah's consternation, but continued: 'It is a little celebration, you understand? He has told you, has he not, of this most excellent appointment in the United States?' She hugged herself delightedly. 'Oh, can you not imagine how wonderful it will be, señorita, living in such an exciting city? Meeting so many interesting people? There will be so much to do – so many places to go! I was becoming bored with London, and I can't wait to get away. Carlos has said we are to have a house on Long Island, and Eduardo will learn to swim and have other children to play with—'

She broke off suddenly as she became aware of Susannah's dismayed expression. 'What is the matter, señorita?' she demanded. 'Are you not pleased that my husband has gained this promotion? Why are you looking so – so miserable?'

Susannah tried to compose herself. 'Nothing's wrong, señora,' she denied. 'So you're going out this evening to celebrate.'

'Have I not just said so?' Lucie looked annoyed. 'Is there something wrong in that? Surely you do not object to staying in this evening, señorita?'

'No. No, of course not, señora.'

Susannah shook her head trying not to feel too disappointed. There was always tomorrow evening, and it was something to look forward to.

Lucie's nostrils flared. 'If you have made arrangements for this evening, *señorita*, then you must change them to tomorrow!'

Susannah nodded. 'Very well, *señora*.'

Lucie gave her one last impatient stare and then turned and left the room. Obviously she considered Susannah's attitude lacking. She had no doubt expected some enthusiasm about the proposed move to New York, but Susannah couldn't think about that now. For the present her thoughts were obsessed with the desire to get to a telephone and tell Fernando Cuevas that she would have dinner with him the following evening.

CHAPTER THREE

IN fact, Susannah did not get to speak to Fernando on the telephone. When she rang his hotel that afternoon, the receptionist politely informed her that Señor Cuevas was out and could she take a message. As Susannah could not be sure of being able to telephone at some other time she had to leave a message with the girl, but it was an unsatisfactory arrangement and she hoped it would reach him. She spent the evening chafing at the restriction she had placed on herself by deciding not to involve anyone else which prevented her from making any call from the Castana house.

On Saturdays, Eduardo had lessons in the morning as usual, but in the afternoon if his father was at home he was taken out by his parents. It gave Susannah a couple of hours to go shopping or attend to her own personal affairs and this week she decided to wash her hair. It was thick and long and took some time to dry, but she used no hair-dryer, allowing it to dry naturally on a towel about her shoulders. Newly washed, it was smooth and silky and she decided that tonight she would leave it loose.

It was not until Eduardo was in bed and she was changing in her room that she realized that no actual arrangement for meeting Fernando had been made. She decided to go to the end of the terrace as before and hoped that her employers would not notice that she appeared to be walking out in a long dress.

It had taken her some time to decide what to wear. At first she had considered wearing trousers. She had several pairs of trousers that looked good when combined with a smock or a lurex tunic, but a feline desire to display a certain femininity forbade such casual attire. Instead she was wearing an amber-coloured caftan, edged with blue and green lurex braid, that dipped deeply to the cleft of her breasts in front and had wide sleeves that displayed her slender arms to advantage. She wore little make-up, adding only a green eye-shadow and a colourless lustre to her lips. Gold hoops swung out from the ashen fairness of her hair and she knew she was looking her best.

As it was a cool evening, she wore a navy blue velvet cape over her dress as she hurried towards the corner just before eight o'clock. As before there was no sign of her escort, and she linked her arms under the cape praying that he had received her message and that he did intend meeting her.

By ten past eight she was feeling chilled to the bone, and it wasn't entirely due to the cold air about her. Where could he be? Should she go and find a telephone and ring his hotel? Perhaps he had not received her message after all. Perhaps he had left for Spain a day earlier than planned!

The horror that this aroused in her frightened her a little. She was allowing things to get out of hand. Heavens, she had only been out with the man once. She could hardly count that visit to the zoo as an invitation to *her*. And never at any time had he given her reason to suppose that he found her more than ordinarily attractive.

At twenty minutes past eight she gave up hope. He wasn't coming and she hadn't the courage to ring his hotel and find out why. She turned miserably and began walking slowly back along the terrace. Perhaps she would be able to slip indoors again without the Castañas knowing. The last thing she wanted was to have to explain why her evening had ended before it had even begun.

She had taken only a few steps when a voice that she ought not to have been so overwhelmingly aware of shouted: 'Susannah! Susannah! *Por dios*, I thought I would miss you!'

She turned rather unsteadily. Fernando was leaping out of the gold Granada at the kerb, running towards her. She stood motionless, unable to show either delight or dismay at his sudden appearance, a choking emotion threatening to devastate her.

'I'm sorry, I'm sorry,' he was saying, a smile in his

39

voice. 'Your London traffic is – how do you say it – *el diablo, si?* I have been stuck in a jam for the best part of forty minutes, and—' He broke off, suddenly becoming aware of her quivering immobility. '*Que?* What is it? Susannah – what is wrong?' He lifted her chin with his fingers looking down into her eyes penetratingly. '*Dios!* You are upset! I am a clumsy fool, am I not? But you knew I would come – surely you knew that!'

Susannah couldn't trust herself not to give her feelings away. She drew her chin away from his hand and made an indifferent little movement of her shoulders. 'How am I supposed to know anything?' she demanded unsteadily.

His dark brows drew together in a frown. 'But of course you knew. Why else would I have issued the invitation?' He reached for her impatiently, his fingers closing over the fine bones of her shoulders, his rings digging into her flesh, giving her a little shake. 'Do you not know how frustrated I felt, sitting in the car, unable to contact you?'

He was close, too close. His body was only inches away from hers. His warm breath was fanning her forehead. Had her hands not been trapped within the enveloping folds of her cape she felt sure she would not have been able to prevent herself from reaching out and touching him. Instead, she looked up into his face. There was concern in the fine darkness of his eyes with their fringing of thick black lashes, concern and something else, something that caused a sudden breathlessness, a sudden inexplicable weakness in her legs.

'*Sagrada Maria,* Susannah!' he muttered huskily, 'do not look at me like that! Do not make me do something we would both regret!'

Her face flamed and she would have pulled away from him, but he shook his head a trifle grimly and with a kind of rough determination propelled her towards the car. Once inside, she averted her head and he got in beside her without a word, driving away from the quiet terrace with his usual expertise.

As they turned into the main stream of traffic he spoke

again. He had evidently got himself well under control, and his voice was cool as he said: 'I suggest we dine at my hotel. It's a little late to be leaving London, do you not think so?'

Susannah made no response and he took her silence to mean acquiescence. They drove through the busy streets thronged with theatre-goers, down Shaftesbury Avenue and into the Strand. Susannah had never been into the Savoy before, and she was glad now that she had chosen to wear a long dress. Fernando for his part seemed totally unimpressed by his surroundings, but in his expensively-cut charcoal lounge suit, a dark red shirt and tie giving him a somewhat alien air, he slotted effortlessly into this background.

He left her for a moment in the reception hall to speak to a man who looked like a manager of some sort. When he came back he put his hand beneath her elbow and led her towards the lift. She looked at him with startled eyes and his expression relaxed a little.

'I thought we might dine in my suite, Susannah,' he explained quietly. 'Do you have any objections?'

Susannah sought about in her mind for a suitable reply. She felt sure that in Spain he would never dream of taking a woman to dine in his suite, but she didn't know how to make the protest.

'Is – is there something wrong with dining in the restaurant?' she inquired unevenly.

'No.' Fernando halted, looking down at her. 'Would you prefer that?'

Susannah pressed her lips together rather unhappily. If she was honest she would admit that she would not prefer that at all. But what respect could he have for a woman who would agree to dine in his suite?

Now, she licked her lips and said: 'If you would – rather not be seen with me—'

She had never seen anyone look so angry. Without a word, he turned and walked back across the reception area, leaving her again while he spoke to the man she had thought was the manager. Then he came back to her. She had shed her cape, but not even the attractiveness of her

41

appearance lifted the cold anger from his eyes.

The next hour was the worst period of Susannah's young life. The exceptional quality of the food was lost on her, and she noticed that Fernando ate little himself, merely drinking liberally of the wine and making a pretence of enjoying the steak and salad he had chosen. She was unutterably relieved when it was over and he suggested they should leave the restaurant.

In the reception area again, she collected her cape and looked at him nervously. 'If – if you'd rather not take me home, *señor*, I shall quite understand,' she murmured, in a small voice.

There was silence for a few moments and then she heard him heave a deep sigh. 'I'm sorry, Susannah,' he said, and she thought he sounded strained. 'I've been – how do you say it – a *pig* all evening!' He shook his head, running a hand round the back of his neck, and tugging at the hair on his nape. 'How will you ever forgive me?'

Susannah trembled. 'It was my fault—' she began, but he interrupted her.

'No, it was mine. You were quite right to refuse my invitation. It would have been a – dangerous situation, and you were right to avoid it. I am sorry.'

Susannah's eyes were wide as she stared at him, and with an exclamation, he said: 'Come! I will take you home. I have an early start in the morning.'

Susannah hung back now. His words chilled her more than his attitude all evening had done, even though they were spoken with warmth and gentleness. Without moving, she looked all about her and said: 'What an attractive building this is. I've never been here before. Does it accommodate a lot of people?'

'A reasonable number,' he remarked dryly. 'And surely you know that as well as I do.'

'Yes.' Susannah still lingered. 'You said you had a suite. What does that consist of?'

Fernando ran his palm down his shirt front, unconsciously drawing Susannah's attention to the fact that he wore nothing beneath it. 'A suite can consist of many rooms or only a few,' he replied briefly.

'Does your suite have many rooms?'

Fernando adjusted the knot of his tie. 'Does it matter?' Then, as her eyes clouded, he added: 'I have a small suite – two bedrooms, a lounge, a bathroom. Does that satisfy you?'

Susannah looked down at her hands. 'Could I see it?'

There was another pregnant silence, and finally Fernando said: 'I don't think that would be a very good idea, Susannah,' in terse tones.

She looked up. 'You sound – angry. Why?'

Fernando took her arm impatiently. 'It's time we were leaving, Susannah. Come along. I'll take you home.'

Susannah made no further demur. Her small spurt of recklessness had been extinguished, and she wished she had not been so foolish. In the car, she stole a surreptitious glance at her watch. Was it only a quarter to ten? It seemed much longer than ninety minutes since she had been waiting so eagerly for him to come.

He drove away from the hotel and along the Embankment. Susannah could see the shadows on the river, and on the opposite bank there were the lights of the Festival Hall. The muted sounds of a ship's siren sounded mournfully across the water and she shivered. Its sad lament suited her mood. Since leaving the hotel Fernando had said nothing at all, and she was overpoweringly aware that she had quickly destroyed his momentary sense of contrition at the boorishness of his behaviour. After tonight she would probably never see him again, and she couldn't help but think that he would be glad to be rid of her.

In a very short time they were drawing up in Lorrimer Terrace and Susannah waited impatiently for the car to stop so that she could get out. Misery cloaked her like an almost physical presence, and she couldn't understand why this man, whom she had known less than a week, should have become so important to her. He didn't care about her, that was obvious. He might find her physically attractive, that she had to accept, as witness his suggestion that they should dine in his suite that evening; but it had been a fleeting attraction which had not survived

43

more than an hour in her company, and she burned with humiliation when she recalled how afterwards she had practically invited him to take advantage of her.

As soon as the car drew to a halt, she reached for the door handle, but was stayed when he said quietly: 'Just one minute, Susannah. Please.'

She sat back in her seat, withdrawing her hand inside her cape again, glad of its concealing folds to hide her trembling nervousness. Her companion switched off the engine, and sat in silence for a few moments. Then he half turned towards her, one arm along the back of her seat.

'I can't let you go like this,' he said, in a low voice. 'I know I've been a brute this evening, but—' He shook his head. 'I ought not to have invited you out again. It's all my fault. I'm sorry if I've made you miserable.'

Susannah's throat felt choked. The last thing she had expected was for him to apologize to her. 'That – that's all right,' she managed. 'I – I shouldn't have accepted.'

'Oh, *Susannah*!' He looked across at her in the gloom, and she could see the glitter of his eyes. 'What can I say? What can I do? I'm leaving tomorrow. There is no time to show you that I mean what I say.'

'Oh, please . . .' Susannah was near to tears, and they would be the final humiliation. 'Thank – thank you for a pleasant evening – *oh*!'

She broke off on a gasp as she felt his fingers against her neck, under the weight of her hair. They moved with a certain sureness to her throat, releasing the catch of her cape so that he could slide it from her shoulders. Then he moved a little closer, uttering an imprecation in his own language at the barrier caused by the gear console.

Susannah remained perfectly still, not looking at him, not making any attempt to encourage or discourage him. She didn't believe this was really happening. Even when she felt the heat of his body through the silk of his shirt that brushed her arm, she told herself that she was exaggerating his nearness. She couldn't really feel the pressure of his thigh against hers, or smell the faint aroma of shaving lotion and tobacco that clung to his clothes. And yet it seemed real enough, and there was another scent, too –

the warm male scent of his body that seemed to be reaching out and enveloping her in a warm and intimate atmosphere. She trembled. She had to be sensible about this. Just because she was experiencing the most wanton desires towards this man she must not imagine that he felt the same way towards her.

'Susannah.' His breath warmed her ear. 'Look at me. Please – look at me.'

She looked. He was closer. She wasn't imagining it. When she turned her face, his was only inches away. The light from the street lamp outside showed the naked hunger in his eyes, the sensual curve of his mouth. With one hand he cupped her cheek, his thumb moving probingly against her lips, caressing them, parting them. Then he bent his head and put his mouth to those parted lips, kissing her gently, exploringly, until something seemed to fuse between them and he could no longer deny his need of her. His hand slid down to her throat, and the pressure of his mouth became an urgent force that impelled her back against the soft upholstery.

'*Te deseo*, Susannah, *de mi alma*,' he whispered, releasing her lips to seek the hollow between her breasts. 'Forgive me, forgive me, but I cannot help myself—'

Susannah's hands came up around his neck, curling into the thick vitality of his hair. She drew his mouth back to hers, returning his kisses with innocent abandon, and not until he dragged himself away from her to slump heavily over the steering wheel did she realize that she had been behaving in a manner tantamount to begging him to make love to her.

With shaking fingers she gathered up her cape, fumbled the door open and stumbled out, slamming it behind her. Then she ran across the pavement and up the steps and into the Castana house. She could hear sounds of music from the drawing-room, but there was no one about, and she ran weakly up the stairs, not stopping until she had reached the safety of her own room. Then she alowed the cape to fall to the floor and threw herself upon her bed to sob uncontrollably . . .

45

On Sunday morning, she felt distinctly unwell. Her head throbbed from the amount of weeping she had done the night before, and her eyes were red-rimmed and haggard. She deliberately applied a heavy make-up before meeting the rest of the household, but that didn't stop Lucie Castana from commenting on her appearance.

'Were you so late yesterday evening, *señorita*?' she exclaimed, examining Susannah's dark-ringed eyes. 'My husband thought he heard you come in soon after ten o'clock.'

'He did.' Susannah made a casual gesture. 'I – I didn't sleep very well, *señora*. I – I think I may have a cold coming on.'

Lucie Castana raised her dark eyebrows. 'Then I trust you will not breathe your germs all over Eduardo, *señorita*, or indeed over the rest of us. You must stay in your room if you feel unwell.'

'Yes, *señora*.' Susannah was resigned. In truth that was exactly what she wanted to do.

'In any case,' continued her employer, 'my husband and I are taking Eduardo out again today. As Carlos is so soon to leave this country, we have friends to visit – to whom we must bid *adios* for the present.'

'Yes, *señora*.'

'We will be leaving in an hour or so. If you are fit when we return home, I shall expect you to put Eduardo to bed as usual, *señorita*.'

'Yes, *señora*.'

The house was quiet after the Castanas had left. The servants, the cook-housekeeper and the maid, had been given the rest of the day off, too, and Susannah had been left a cold lunch in the dining-room should she require it. Mrs. Travers, the cook-housekeeper, left soon after her employers. She had a sister in Ealing, and Susannah speculated that she was probably going there. Eleanor, the maid, left a little later, but as Susannah knew very little about her, she had no idea where she might be going. She supposed in other circumstances she could have been friendly with Eleanor, who was about her own age, but a governess's position in a household was still a nebulous one, accepted neither upstairs nor downstairs, as it were.

At about eleven o'clock she went down to the kitchen to make herself a cup of coffee. Now that she was alone she felt restless and every aircraft that passed overhead reminded her that this morning Fernando would be on a flight for Madrid. She wondered what part of Spain he came from – where he lived – what he did. She would never know now . . .

Forcing herself to think about other things, she began considering the Castanas' eventual move to New York. Did she want to go with them, or would she prefer to remain in England and take another post? Taking another post would mean getting used to a new routine, making friends with a new child, or children, settling into another household. Was that what she wanted to do? Or ought she to take the advice of her best friend and think seriously of settling down and getting married?

Thinking of her friend, Susannah moved towards the hall and the telephone. She and Margaret French had been at college together, but Margaret had barely arrived in London and settled into a job before meeting a fellow teacher and getting married. Now she had a two-year-old baby daughter, Toni, and Susannah was as welcome in their home in Kennington as any of their own relatives. She decided to telephone Margaret and ask whether they would give her lunch if she came over. She knew without conceit they'd be delighted. It was almost three weeks since she had seen them.

But even as she reached for the receiver the phone began to ring and she stifled a startled cry before answering it. She gave the number and was about to tell whoever was calling that Señor and Señora Castana were away for the day when a deep masculine voice said: 'Susannah! Susannah, is that you?'

Her legs gave way under her and she sought the support of a polished chest nearby. '*Fernando!*' she breathed in astonishment, unconscious of the fact that she was using his Christian name. 'But – where are you?'

'Susannah! Oh, it is good to hear your voice again.'

47

'Fernan – I mean–' She halted uncertainly as the initial shock of hearing his voice began to wear off. 'Señor Cuevas – where are you calling from?'

'It was Fernando a moment ago,' he reproved her gently. 'I much prefer that.'

She was glad he could not witness her embarrassment. 'But how can you be telephoning me? I – I thought you would have been on the plane by now.'

There was a moment's silence and she thought at first that he had rung off, but then he said quietly: 'My flight left over an hour ago, Susannah.'

Susannah gasped, 'What?'

'You heard what I said.' He sounded suddenly impatient. 'But now – how was I lucky enough to reach you immediately? Where are your employers?'

'Señor and Señora Castana have gone out for the day. They won't be back until early this evening.'

'Is that so?' He sounded very interested. 'And you are free?'

'I – I suppose so.'

'You sound – reluctant.' There was concern in his voice now. 'Do you not wish to see me again after last night?'

'Oh – Fernando!' She heaved a tremulous sigh. 'Of course I want to see you. What do you want me to do?'

He hesitated. 'I am telephoning from my hotel. I will get a taxi and be with you in – say – fifteen minutes?'

'All right.'

After she had hung up the receiver she sat for a moment staring down at her hands and then she became galvanized into action. She rushed up the stairs to her room and went straight to look at her reflection in the bathroom mirror. The thick make-up she had applied looked caked on her face and with an exclamation she ran some water into the basin and scrubbed it all off with a face-cloth. Then she looked at herself again, still most dissatisfied with what she could see. Whatever would he think of her? She looked an absolute hag!

Turning from the mirror, she went into her bedroom and stripped off the skirt and blouse she had been wearing. She took a pair of lemon slacks from her wardrobe and tugged them on, and then added a cream chunky sweater. She looked a pale reflection of herself, and taking the brush she tugged it viciously through her hair, dispersing some of her frustration in the deliberate masochism.

The doorbell rang as she was applying a blue eye-shadow and she glanced quickly at her watch. It was only between ten and twelve minutes since his call. It couldn't be Fernando already – could it?

She was by no means ready to face him yet. Her cheeks were still without make-up of any kind and she had planned to apply a light rouge to give herself some artificial colour. She sighed. Whoever it was, it couldn't be for her. They would probably go away if she didn't answer.

The bell rang again, insistently, as though someone was deliberately keeping their finger pressed on it. She would have to go. After all, it could be something important. She put down the brush she had been using, and with a resigned gesture at her reflection went out of her bedroom and down the stairs to the hall. By now whoever was calling was growing impatient and the bell was ringing continuously.

She unlocked the heavy door and opened it cautiously, stepping back in amazement when she saw who it was. 'Fernando!' she gasped. 'How did you get here so soon?'

He came in without speaking, his eyes eloquent with feeling. He closed the door behind him and then stood looking at her. Susannah felt terrible. What must he be thinking? She had not even finished brushing her hair.

'I – I'm sorry—' she began. 'I – I thought it must be someone else—'

And then she was in his arms, her hands were imprisoned against his chest, and his mouth sought the parted sweetness of hers. She had never been so close to him before. In the car they had been separated by the gear console and only the upper part of his body had been against her. But now she could feel the lean strength of him, and as his hands slid down to her hips to bring her

49

closer she was made irresistibly aware of his stirring masculinity. His jacket was fastened at first, but he unbuttoned it and she yielded against him, sliding her arms around his waist and making little involuntary sounds of pleasure.

At last he propelled her away from him, holding her at arm's length even though she protested and tried to wriggle close to him again. 'Susannah,' he muttered urgently. 'We must be sensible about this. I want to make love to you very much, but not in the hall of the house of Carlos Castana!'

Susannah came to her senses in an agony of self-consciousness. 'I – of course,' she said jerkily, and he released her. She put up her hands to her hair. 'I – I must look an absolute mess. If you'll excuse me, I'll go and tidy up—'

Fernando drew out his cheroots and lit one with unsteady fingers. 'There is no urgency,' he observed dryly. 'And you do not look a mess. You look *muy deseable* – very desirable!' He touched the dark rings beneath her eyes. 'But you did not sleep well last night, did you?'

She half turned away, not wanting his compassion. 'Not very well.'

He caught her wrist. 'I, also, did not sleep well.'

'Oh!' She made a helpless gesture. 'I'm sorry. I – I'll just go and finish making up—'

He uttered an expletive, and his fingers tightly perceptibly on her wrist. 'Forget about your appearance,' he commanded quietly. '*No importa!* Only you are important.'

'Am I?' She sounded unconvinced.

'*Condenacion!* Of course you are!' He sighed, looking at her almost diffidently. 'Susannah, I am finding this very hard, but I must explain to you why I could not leave this morning—'

'There's no need.'

'There's every need.' His jaw was taut. 'Susannah, no matter what you may think of me, I am not in the habit of indulging in promiscuous affairs. I have never done this sort of thing before—'

'Oh, please—'

'No. Let me continue. I have to tell you why I behaved as I did last night and again this morning—'

'Fernando, forget it—'

'No, I will not forget it!' He scowled and she thought how alien he suddenly appeared. 'Susannah, you are deliberately misunderstanding me. I do not know what you expect me to say, but in my country a man does not defile a young, unmarried woman without feeling the need for self-recrimination.'

Susannah didn't know how to answer him. She didn't know what he was trying to say, it was true, but somehow she imagined he was about to destroy all the joy she had felt when first he telephoned her.

'Fernando, things are different in England. I – girls – people kiss one another without there having to be a federal case about it—'

'Be silent!' He sounded furious. 'Is that how you regard this – this lovemaking between us? *Kissing?* Have you let other men hold you as I held you? Let other men kiss you as I kissed you?'

Susannah's breathing was constricted. 'I didn't say that.'

'Then what are you saying?'

She dragged herself away from him, rubbing her wrist as the sudden releasing of his fingers allowed the blood to course tinglingly down into her hand. 'I – I just don't want you to feel that you have to apologize for something that was no more your fault than mine,' she murmured bitterly.

'An apology?' He pressed out his cheroot savagely in the ashtray on the chest. 'Is that how you see it, Susannah?'

She turned away defeatedly, moving towards the stairs. 'I – I won't be a minute—' she began unsteadily, but he came after her, his hands grasping her shoulders, pulling her irresistibly back against him. For a few moments she struggled, but when his mouth sought the warm curve of her neck she surrendered to the desire to submit to something that was stronger than self-respect.

'Susannah,' he groaned in a tortured voice, 'I did not

come here to apologize. I came because I had to. I had to see you again, do you understand? *Amada*, I don't want to hurt you, but you have – how do you say it – penetrated my skin? I am in love with you.'

Susannah couldn't believe her ears. Even though the possession in his hands about her waist was reassuringly real, she could not accept that he had actually said he loved her.

'Fernando?' she breathed questioningly, and with an exclamation he turned her in his arms so that his mouth could find hers once more.

Eventually he had to pull away from her again, but this time she felt no sense of shame or withdrawal at his parting. It was intoxicating to know that she could arouse this man in such a way that he had no defence against her. A smile touched her lips at these secret thoughts and seeing her expression he said dryly: 'You find it amusing?'

Susannah was contrite, and she went close to him, fingering the lapels of his coat, looking up at him appealingly. 'No, not amusing,' she denied softly. 'Just – just wonderful, that's all.'

Fernando's fingers lingered on her upper arms, but he was determined in his efforts to keep her away from him. 'Susannah,' he said, huskily, 'I don't think you are wearing anything under that sweater, and the temptation to find out becomes stronger by the moment. Please, allow me to remain in control of the situation!'

Susannah's cheeks burned, and now he smiled, smoothing a hand over his hair, fastening the buttons of his jacket.

'Go and get a coat,' he said quietly, giving her a gentle push. 'We will go and have some lunch and then you can show me some peaceful part of your city where we can be alone together, *si*?'

CHAPTER FOUR

THEY had lunch at an out-of-the-way little restaurant in Soho. Fernando had chosen a Greek establishment this time, and they ate *moussaka*, sliced aubergines and minced meat in a thick sauce, and veal cutlets served with a green salad. They talked desultorily throughout the meal, relaxed casual conversations concerning impersonal topics, and only when their eyes met across the table did the communication between them become intimate and disturbing.

Afterwards, they walked for a while. Fernando had dismissed his hired car the previous evening, so they were confined to taxicabs for transportation. But Susannah liked walking. She liked the sensation of Fernando's strong fingers enclosing hers, and the way the light breeze lifted his straight dark hair depositing a thick swathe across his forehead. The brightness of the day seemed to reflect her mood, and she thought she had never felt happier. Neither of them had spoken so far of Fernando's eventual return to Spain. For Susannah, it was sufficient at present to know that he had stayed because of her.

Towards teatime they found a quiet corner beneath the trees in Kensington Gardens and sat down upon the grass. It was a favourite rendezvous for lovers, and they attracted no especial attention. Fernando rested back upon his elbows, and Susannah drew up her legs and wrapped her arms around her knees. The day was almost over and now a sense of anti-climax was developing, threatening to overwhelm her.

Fernando stretched out a hand, touching her shoulder and drawing her back beside him. 'Now what are you thinking?' he demanded, scanning her troubled features. 'Have you not enjoyed yourself today?'

Susannah relaxed back against the soft turf, warmed by the unusual heat of the sun. 'I've had a wonderful day,

Fernando,' she murmured, rather wistfully. 'But it's almost over.'

He rested on an elbow looking down at her, 'Ah, I understand,' he said softly. 'You do not wish it to end?' He shook his head. 'Nor do I.' He glanced at his watch. 'But there are hours yet—'

'No!' She tried to prop herself up. 'No, I have to be back before seven. Señora Castana expects me to put Eduardo to bed.'

Fernando's mouth turned down at the corners. 'Cannot Lucie Castana put her own child to bed for once?' he exclaimed.

Susannah sighed. 'She asked me to do it. I – I have to go back. It's my job, after all.'

Fernando uttered an impatient ejaculation. 'And tomorrow, of course, you will be working?'

'Tomorrow?' she faltered.

'*Si, mañana.*'

'But – but—' She licked her lips. 'Won't you be – that is – I thought you had to return to – to Spain.'

Fernando's eyes narrowed, the thick lashes veiling his expression. 'Do you wish me to return to Spain tomorrow, Susannah?'

'Oh, no, *no!*' She reached towards him, stroking his cheek with her fingers. 'I – I don't want you to return at all,' she confessed honestly.

Fernando covered her hand with his own, turning her palm to his lips, kissing each of her fingers with nerve-shattering tenderness. 'I shall not be returning to Spain tomorrow,' he stated huskily. 'I shall telegraph them that I have been – delayed.'

'Oh, Fernando!'

Susannah's lips parted tremulously and with a muffled groan he bent over her, seeking her mouth and exploring it with his own until passion flared between them. The the weight of his body was a disruptive pressure that destroyed her defences, causing her own body to become soft and yielding, arching against him, inviting his possession . . .

'What are you doing?'

The high, childish voice caused Fernando to draw back from Susannah with reluctance, looking over his shoulder impatiently at the small girl who was standing watching them. He jack-knifed into a sitting position, and while Susannah tried to gather her scattered senses he raked a hand through his hair and said sharply: 'Ought you to be speaking to strangers, *pequeña*?' in peculiarly taut tones. 'Where is your mama?'

As though in answer to his question, they could now hear a woman's voice shouting: 'Linda! Linda, where are you? Come here at once, you naughty girl!'

Linda, for that was obviously her name, gave Fernando a rather impudent grin and then darted away between the trees in the direction of her mother's voice.

But the incident had had a curious effect on Fernando, for now, without looking at Susannah, he rose to his feet, dusting himself down and saying: 'Perhaps we should be going for some tea, *si*? Then I will take you home.'

Susannah scrambled to her feet, brushing the blades of grass from her trousers. She wondered why his mood had changed so drastically. Surely a child's innocent curiosity was not wholly responsible for that grim line around his mouth.

They had tea and scones at a coffee bar in Knightsbridge and then Fernando hailed a cab to take them to Lorrimer Terrace. They had spoken little since that incident in the park and Susannah was beginning to feel that awful sense of anti-climax again. What was wrong? Why was he so – withdrawn?

The taxi halted outside the Castana house and Susannah climbed out before he could stop her. However, asking the taxi driver to wait, Fernando climbed out also, halting her at the foot of the steps. 'Will I see you tomorrow?' he demanded, possessing himself of her hands.

Susannah was confused. 'Do – do you want to?'

'Do you doubt it?' Fernando's lips thinned.

She shook her head. 'I don't know what to think. I – I thought you had changed your mind.'

Fernando sighed, raising her hands to his lips. 'I'm

sorry,' he said huskily. 'And I haven't changed – not at all.' He glanced round impatiently at the waiting taxi. 'Tomorrow evening, *si*?'

'All right,' Susannah nodded.

'The usual arrangement.' He smiled. 'I will endeavour not to be late.' He bent his head to her fingers again. *'Te adoro, mi alma. Hasta mañana!'* Then he turned and left her, climbing into the taxi without a backward glance, leaving her feeling oddly tearful.

Susannah saw Fernando every evening of the week that followed. Fortunately the Castanas were so wrapped up in their own affairs that they paid little attention to her movements and consequently she was not obliged to make any awkward explanations. It was a time of nervous excitement for Susannah, living her days in eager anticipation of the evening to come, and then spending the latter half of the evening worrying in case Fernando had decided to return to Spain the next day.

Their meetings were all in public places. They spent very little time alone. Susannah thought this was a deliberate ploy on Fernando's behalf. He knew better than she did how easy it would be for their relationship to develop into dangerous intimacies and she suspected that he respected her too much to take advantage of her. All the same, the brief kisses in the cab taking her home were an unsatisfactory substitute for what she knew to be his wholly passionate lovemaking, and she cried herself to sleep at nights, aching with a hunger that only he could assuage.

But on Friday evening, sitting in the comfortable smoky atmosphere of a pub they had frequented in Chelsea, he said: 'How does the idea of a week-end in the country appeal to you, Susannah?'

He was looking particularly attractive this evening in a cream lounge suit and a bronze patterned shirt, and she had been sitting looking steadily into his eyes, sharing in that intangible communication the kind of mounting awareness that physically they denied themselves.

Now, she blinked and said: 'A week-end in the

56

country? Why?'

Fernando moved closer to her on the high-backed banquette that gave an added privacy to their secluded corner of the bar. 'A friend of mine – a business colleague, if you like – owns a cottage in a place called Wendcombe, do you know it?'

'Wendcombe?' Susannah frowned, trying to ignore the trembling sensation that was assailing her. 'Vaguely. It – it's a village, isn't it? In Buckinghamshire?'

'That sounds familiar – Buckinghamshire. *Si*, I am sure that is the word he used.' Fernando nodded. '*Bien* – does a week-end at this cottage sound appealing to you?'

Susannah could feel her cheeks beginning to burn. 'I don't quite know what you mean—' she began unsteadily.

'Don't you?' He looked at her and his face was very close to hers. 'I think you do, Susannah.'

She quivered. 'You mean – spend a week-end at this cottage – with you – alone?'

His eyes narrowed. 'Is that such a daunting proposition, Susannah?'

She caught her breath. Daunting was not a word she would have used. Provocative, reckless, dangerous even – they were words she would have used.

She dragged her gaze away from his and stared down into her glass. How was she to answer him? How could she tell him that she had never done such a thing before? Did he perhaps think she had? Had her response to him in some way influenced his decision to ask her? Didn't he realize that no man had ever aroused her as he had aroused her? Or was he of the opinion that all young Englishwomen indulged in permissive sex?

She darted a glance at him. He was staring down into his glass and there was a curiously vulnerable sag to his shoulders. What was he thinking? What answer did he expect her to give? Did he expect her to refuse?

All week he had taken her to busy night spots, and never once had he attempted to make love to her. Even the kisses he had given her in the cab going home had been tender and circumspect. And now this . . .

57

She drew a deep breath. During this week she had learned only a little more about him. She now knew that his family owned vineyards in the southern part of Spain, near Cadiz, and that he was in London on business to do with the exporting of the wine they produced. But that was all. He had told her nothing about his personal affairs, although she imagined he thought he had told her all that was necessary. There was no doubt that he loved her – it was there in every touch of their hands, every gentle kiss bestowed upon her cheeks, every look they shared that intimated at the satisfaction they would share if ever she surrendered completely to him. And she had fondly imagined that sooner or later their relationship would develop into a more binding contract. But not like this . . .

Taking her elbows from where they had been resting on the table in front of them, she said quietly: 'I – I couldn't do that, Fernando.'

There was silence for a while as he absorbed this, not moving from his hunched position. Then he lay back against the soft upholstery, his mouth twisting. 'Very well.' He looked towards the bar. 'Would you like another drink?'

Susannah gave a helpless little exclamation. 'Fernando – try to understand. I – I couldn't—'

'You do not have to go on, Susannah. I quite understand.' He swallowed the remainder of the whisky in his glass, considering its emptiness thoughtfully. 'Excuse me. I need another drink.'

He walked across to the counter and she watched him. He moved easily, lithely, and quite a number of women turned to look after him. His clothes fitted him closely with the evident cut of good tailoring and his hair always looked newly washed and smooth. To seriously consider spending a week-end with him – imagining him without his excellently tailored suits, lean and tanned, his hair tousled from sleep, making love to her – could not be so carelessly dismissed. Other girls went in for that sort of thing and with men much less attractive than Fernando Cuevas. Men they did not even love – and Susannah was sure she loved Fernando ... And he loved her ... or could he, to ask such a thing?

By the time he came back her palms were moist, and there was a terrible feeling of inadequacy invading her stomach. She was such a coward. She was so afraid of what might happen. Was she going to risk the same consequences as her mother and possibly find herself alone and pregnant by a man who had quickly disappeared after getting what he wanted?

But would Fernando desert her? He had said he loved her. She didn't believe he had made that up. She *couldn't* believe it. So where did that leave her? If she refused him, would she ever see him again? Or was this in the nature of an ultimatum?

He came and sat beside her again, raising his glass to her in a silent salute. Then he replaced it on the table and sought about for his cheroots and lighter. When a cheroot was lit, and he had inhaled deeply, he said: 'I have something to tell you, Susannah. I must return to Spain at the beginning of next week.'

Susannah felt numb. She had known it would have to come – eventually. But so soon! She felt almost ill with reaction.

Forcing her lips to move, she spoke rather stiffly: 'I see. I – I shall miss you.'

He half turned towards her. 'And I shall miss you,' he told her roughly. 'You don't know how much.'

She was breathing jerkily. 'Do – do you have to go?'

'I'm afraid so.' He turned away from her again, drawing almost impatiently on his cheroot. 'You have made my stay in London very – memorable.'

Susannah found it hard to swallow. 'Is that all?' she whispered.

He gave her a sideways glance. 'What do you expect me to say?'

She shook her head. 'Will – will I see you again?'

'Maybe.' He looked down at the glowing tip of his cheroot. 'Maybe the next time I come to London – if you are still living with the Castanas.'

Susannah gasped. 'But the Castanas are leaving

London. They're going to live in New York. They – they've asked me to go with them.'

His brows drew together in a scowl. 'And are you going?'

'I – I don't know.' She shivered at the look in his eyes. 'I've told them I need time to – to think about it.'

His fingers closed over her wrist, and quite suddenly his thigh was pressing against hers. 'Susannah,' he muttered violently, '*please* – come to Wendcombe with me. I want so much to be with you – alone with you – away from all these people. I want to share this week-end with you – I want to show you how much I love you!' His lips caressed her ear. 'And you want it, too. You know you do.'

Susannah was trembling quite uncontrollably now. 'Fernando,' she began half-heartedly, but the desire to please him, to do as he wanted, was eating away at her puny resolution.

His eyes were warmly compelling, openly sensuous. He stroked his fingers along the veins at the inner side of her wrist. 'You could get away, could you not? I am sure the Castanas would permit you to leave after lunch tomorrow, *si*?'

Susannah drew a shaky breath. 'They – they might . . .'

He cupped her chin with his hand. 'Are you afraid of me, Susannah? You have no need to be. I will not hurt you. I just want to – worship you, with my body as well as my soul!'

Susannah gave in, leaning against him, needing the reassuring contact of his broad chest. 'I've never – done anything like this before, Fernando,' she confessed, almost inaudibly. 'You – you will have to be patient with me.'

Fernando looked down at her with eyes grown dark with passion. 'I shall be very patient with you, *amada*, have no fear,' he murmured, his gaze lingering on her mouth. 'But now I think we must be going, before I am tempted to show you exactly how much I need you.'

The Castanas were not unduly perturbed when Susannah broached the subject of her being away from

Saturday afternoon until Sunday evening. She hated telling lies, but she had to pretend that she was going to spend the week-end with a girl friend, and that as they were going to be late on Saturday evening her friend had suggested that Susannah should sleep there. Everything went off very smoothly. Eduardo had his lessons as usual on Saturday morning, Susannah's case was already packed, and after an early lunch she did as Fernando had advised and took a taxi to the Savoy.

He met her in the reception hall, dark and attractive in a navy denim suit, and took her case from her unresisting fingers, smiling down into her eyes so that she was warmed to the farthest extremes of her being. 'I, too, am ready,' he told her gently. 'My case is already in the car.'

'A car?' Susannah frowned. 'You have a car?'

'You did not suppose I would take you to some lonely cottage without some means of transport, did you, Susannah?' he chided softly, urging her outside. 'Come along. We are wasting time. I want you – all to myself.'

Fernando had hired a sleek grey Mercedes and Susannah settled into the front seat rather uncertainly. 'Do you not like it?' he asked perceptively. 'I thought you might. I – have a car like this – back home.'

'It's very – sophisticated,' she conceded, glancing round at the enormous back seat. 'But I liked the Granada.'

'Yes, so did I,' he agreed, and then with a shrug, half turned in his seat to reverse out of the parking area.

Driving through the Buckinghamshire countryside, Susannah felt a little of her nervousness leaving her. It was a very comfortable car with limitless reserves of speed, and she could not deny a certain pleasure at the knowledge that he had hired it because of her. All the same, the knowledge that he owned such a car in Spain made her aware that his world was vastly different from hers.

Wendcombe was an attractive village set around a small square with a stretch of green turf and a pond on which ducks splashed with apparent disregard for bystanders. There was a grey stone church, a village store and post office, and a schoolhouse. Apart from that, the buildings were a mixture of tall stone houses and small, whitewashed cottages. The late afternoon sunshine deepened the yellow of nodding daffodils in clutches on the green, and there was a tranquil, unhurried air that was a pleasing contrast to the noisy bustle of the city they had left behind.

'Oh, it's delightful!' exclaimed Susannah, unable to hide her enthusiasm. She turned to Fernando, negotiating the narrow streets with caution. 'Have you been here before?'

He gave her a wry smile. 'Only once before. When Robert and his wife invited me for a week-end. They only use the cottage at week-ends – and not every week-end,' he added meaningfully.

Susannah flushed and sat back in her seat. For a moment, the reason why they were here had been forgotten, but now as full recollection hit her she felt a disturbing sense of apprehension filling her stomach.

Fernando was very perceptive where she was concerned, for he said softly: 'Relax, Susannah. You are here to enjoy yourself. No on one is going to force you to do anything you do not want to do, you know that.'

Wistaria Cottage stood at the end of the village in a little walled garden. The mild weather had caused the climbing shrub which gave the cottage its name to burgeon with blossom and little clusters of purple and blue flowers hung by the white-painted door. There was a lane at the side of the cottage where Fernando could leave the car, and a narrow crazy-paved path led between flower beds to the door. Fernando parked the Mercedes, took their cases out of the boot, and pocketed the keys before leading the way up the path. He inserted a key in the lock and then stood aside so that she could precede him into the cottage.

They entered what was obviously the living-room, but a wood-panelled staircase focused attention, and beyond it Susannah could see a smaller dining area. The floors were original, now highly polished and scattered with coloured rugs; there were low beams, and cream-painted walls, and leather furniture which went well with its old-world atmosphere. Horse brasses hung above a wide fire-place where logs had been laid for lighting should it prove cold enough, but even in those first few minutes Susannah appreciated the warmth of a central heating system which had been installed in the most unobtrusive way possible.

She stepped tentatively into the room, looking about her with interest, while Fernando closed the door behind them and stood their cases at the foot of the panelled staircase.

'*Bien?*' he said, at last, just behind her. 'Do you like it?'

She took a few more steps before turning and spreading her arms. 'It's – beautiful. I've heard of people having these kind of week-end places, but I never dreamed that so much could be done so attractively. They haven't altered the place at all really.'

Fernando folded his arms. 'No, you are right. It is most tasteful.'

Susannah took a deep breath. 'Where's the kitchen? Are you hungry? Would you like some tea – coffee?'

Fernando's arms fell to his sides. 'The kitchen is through here. I will show you. And yes, I would like some coffee. But the Cunninghams' housekeeper, a Señora Minto, she will be coming to prepare dinner for us.'

Susannah's face fell. 'Oh! Oh, will she?'

She tried to keep the dismay out of her voice, but she couldn't have succeeded because he said: 'Why? Would you have rather prepared our meal yourself?'

Susannah swallowed with difficulty. 'Well, I mean – won't she think it rather – odd? Us staying here? Alone?'

Fernando looked amused. 'Perhaps,' he conceded, 'but like all good housekeepers, she will keep her thoughts to herself.'

The kitchen, unlike the other downstairs rooms of the cottage, had been extensively modernized and a double-drainer sink unit with lots of fitted shelves under which reposed a washer, tumbler drier, refrigerator and dishwasher put it very definitely into the twentieth century. There was also a waste-disposal system which Susannah had never seen before.

Fernando flicked through fitted cupboards, pointed out coffee, sugar, china, indicated the milk and other fresh foods in the fridge, and then left her to get on with it. She heard him going upstairs and an unexpected feeling of contentment enveloped her. What did it matter what anyone else thought? They were two adult human beings, perfectly free to live their lives as they chose.

When the coffee was ready she carried it into the front room on a tray, putting the tray down on a low table before the fireplace. Fernando was still upstairs, and on impulse Susannah climbed the stairs herself, curious to see the upper floor of the cottage. The stairs gave on to a narrow landing from which four doors opened. One of the doors was ajar and she saw it led into the main bedroom at the front of the house.

She hesitated in the doorway and then saw their two cases reposing side by side on an ottoman at the foot of a large fourposter bed. There was no sign of Fernando in here either, but a door to one side was open and she guessed it led to an adjoining bathroom. The bedroom was carpeted in white tumble-twist, and there was a white patterned spread on the huge bed. The walls were pastel-washed and there were long yellow curtains at the bow windows.

As she hovered in the doorway, Fernando emerged from the bathroom, his jacket slung carelessly over one shoulder. He had obviously been washing and he had taken off his tie and loosened the top two buttons of his purple silk shirt. She could see the beginnings of the dark brown hair that grew round his throat, and her stomach plunged. Even like this it was an absurdly intimate situation.

When he saw her, he flung his jacket over a wooden-armed chair in a corner and came towards her. He halted only about a foot away from her and Susannah panicked.

'Er – your – your coffee's ready,' she stammered, half

afraid of what he was about to do. 'I just wondered where you were . . .'

Her voice trailed away and Fernando considered her troubled expression for several agonizing moments before gesturing at the room behind him. 'Do you want to see the rest of the place?'

Susannah hesitated. 'I – I suppose this is the master bedroom.'

'If, by that, you mean the main bedroom, then yes, that is correct.' His voice was cool, not at all loverlike, and she quivered. 'There is an adjoining bathroom, as you can see, with a shower as well as the usual fittings.'

Susannah nodded. 'It – it's very attractive.' She stepped aside as he came out of the bedroom and opened the next door along the landing.

'This is the second bedroom,' he remarked, and she took a hasty look. There was a lemon carpet in here and blue curtains, and the bed was an ordinary double one.

'Very nice,' she said inadequately.

'The other doors need not concern you. One opens into the bathroom which can be reached from the – main bedroom. The other is a sort of storeroom. Boxroom, I believe Marion called it.'

'Yes.' Susannah forced her stiff lips into a smile. 'Well – shall we go down and have our coffee now?'

Fernando looked at her impatiently. 'Susannah, what have I said? What have I done? You are behaving as if you were afraid I was about to pounce on you! I assure you, I would not dream of forcing my attentions on anyone!'

Susannah moved awkwardly. 'I'm sorry.'

He said something under his breath which she realized was not very complimentary, and then strode to the stairs, going down them two at a time. Susannah followed more slowly, aware that in the circumstances her behaviour must seem quite incomprehensible to him.

Fernando was seated on the leather couch when she reached the living-room, pouring out two cups of coffee with deliberate concentration. He had, she thought purposely, seated himself in the centre of the couch so that to sit beside him she would have had to have asked him to move along. His legs were splayed wide and he lifted his coffee cup broodingly, swallowing its contents without enjoyment. Susannah perched on the edge of an armchair, leaning forward to help herself to cream and sugar. As she stirred the aromatic liquid she looked unhappily at him, but he chose to ignore her, finishing his coffee and replacing his cup on its saucer. Then he rested back against the soft upholstery, his arms stretched along its back on either side of him. The attitude put a strain on the buttons of his shirt and the fine material separated between fastenings giving Susannah a disturbing glimpse of brown skin.

She drank her own coffee and when it was finished rose to take the tray into the kitchen again.

'Leave it!' he ordered abruptly.

'But I thought – if I washed these up – didn't you say someone was coming to cook our dinner?'

His eyes were cold between the thick lashes. 'I said leave it.'

Susannah stared at him uncomfortably, but a sense of resentment at his manner overcame her nervousness. 'I'm not a servant, you know,' she declared, in a rather uneven tone, and bending lifted the tray.

Fernando got to his feet also and for a few moments there was a silent battle of wills. And then, Susannah dragged her gaze away from his and walked determinedly towards the kitchen. He let her go, although she had been half afraid that he wouldn't, but once out of sight of his denigrating stare her courage deserted her. She put down the tray and her shoulders sagged. This wasn't what she wanted – to quarrel with him. She loved him.

She spent as long as she dared washing the dishes and then returned to the living room. Fernando was stretched out on the couch now reading a newspaper and didn't look up when she came in. She sighed. What was she supposed to do? She looked down at the green trousers of the slack suit she had travelled in. She supposed she could take a shower and change. She didn't want to stay in trousers all evening. She had brought a rather attractive hostess gown to wear.

On impulse, she turned and went up the panelled staircase. In the bedroom, she opened her suitcase and took out a towel and her toilet bag. Then she went into the bathroom, relieved to see that she could lock both doors.

The water was beautifully hot, and after securing her hair beneath a shower cap obviously left there for the purpose, she stepped under its soothing stream. It wasn't until she had dried herself that she remembered that she hadn't brought her dress in with her, so wrapping the towel sarong-wise round her body she emerged, carrying her trousers and sweater. Then she stopped short. Fernando was sitting on the side of the bed, his elbows resting on his knees, his head buried in his hands. His whole attitude was one of complete despair, and her heart went out to him. He had obviously not heard her open the bathroom door, but he seemed to sense that he was no longer alone, for he dropped his hands between his knees, looking round at her. Then he sprang to his feet and moved across to the windows, keeping as far away from her as possible. At least, that was what Susannah thought.

She folded her trousers over the back of a chair, laid her sweater on top of them and then turned to her suitcase. But her eyes were irresistibly drawn to Fernando, standing with his back to her, his hands thrust deep into his trousers' pockets. He was staring down into the garden below the windows and she wished she knew what he was thinking.

With a helpless shrug, she took out her dress and went into the bathroom, closing the door but not locking it. The dress was a long one, black with an edging of white, which accentuated the pale silkiness of her hair and the creamy texture of her skin. It had long sleeves, but the neckline was low and round, hinting at the swell at her breasts without revealing anything. The zip proved awkward, but she managed without having to ask his assistance.

In the bedroom again, she brushed her hair briskly and set out her eyeshadow and foundation cream on the dressing table. But after putting down the brush she turned to look at him again and said, on impulse: 'Do you like my dress?'

Fernando turned, and she saw the lines of strain around his mouth. 'It's very beautiful,' he essayed briefly. 'You are very beautiful. But of course, you know that.'

Susannah allowed a little of her own despair to show. 'I'm sorry, Fernando,' she said helplessly. 'I – I'm a fool—'

'*No!*' He interrupted her harshly. 'It is I who am a fool. I should not have brought you here.'

'Why?' Her lips trembled. 'Don't you – want me?'

'*Want you?* He moved then, striding the space between them with grim determination, taking her in his arms and pressing her so close that she was left in no doubt that he wanted her. '*Por dios*, Susannah,' he groaned against her neck, 'I love you, I love you, I love you! I've never loved any woman before – except my mother, and then it was not like this, not urgent and destructive, not tearing me apart because I have no right to hurt you—'

Susannah's arm slid round his neck, her hands caressed him, her fingers slid into his hair, her lips sought every inch of his ears and throat. 'Oh, you're not hurting me, Fernando,' she insisted, meaning every word. 'Only – only when you treat me as you did downstairs. I – I wanted to die!'

Fernando's breathing was swift and shallow, evidence of his emotional upheaval, his mouth more disturbingly sensuous than ever before. His hands slid possessively over her back, seeking the low neckline of her dress, his fingers exploring the small bones of her shoulders. 'I didn't want to hurt you,' he protested thickly. 'But you hurt me, and I hit back. You looked so – so terrified, earlier on. I don't want you to be afraid of me, Susannah. I need you so much. I just want to love you . . .'

Susannah returned his kisses with an abandon that unconsciously revealed that fear was not among the emotions she was feeling towards him now. She clung to him eagerly, and for several minutes they assuaged a little of the hunger they felt towards one another.

Suddenly there was a sound from the room below. It was definitely a door closing, and with resigned reluctance Fernando forced her away from him.

'Señora Minto, one supposes,' he commented huskily, and then turned away from her. '*Cristo*, Susannah, do not look at me like that. I am only a man with weaknesses like other men!'

Susannah's lips curved tenderly. 'I know.'

He glanced back at her, clenching his fists. 'Go downstairs and introduce yourself to the good Señora Minto,' he advised. 'I think now it is my turn to take a shower!'

CHAPTER FIVE

MRS. MINTO was not the martinet Susannah had expected her to be, but nevertheless, she soon made it obvious that she at least did not approve of the Cunninghams lending their cottage to an unmarried couple. Susannah had considered wearing a ring on her third finger, but after meeting Mrs. Minto she was glad she hadn't. Somehow she knew she would have been incapable of deceiving her.

When Susannah first went downstairs she found the housekeeper in the kitchen taking off her overcoat and putting on an apron. She smiled politely when Susannah appeared, and said: 'How do you do, miss. I'm Alice Minto. I believe you're expecting me.'

Susannah relaxed a little. 'Yes, that's right. Hello. I'm Susannah – King.' She glanced round awkwardly. 'It's very kind of you to come and prepare our dinner like this. And on a Saturday, too.'

Mrs. Minto tied the strings of her apron. 'It's my job, miss. When Mr. and Mrs. Cunningham are here, I'm expected to come in Sundays, as well.'

'Oh!' Susannah caught her lower lip between her teeth. 'Do you – I mean – have you everything you need?'

'Yes, miss. I've got the oven on now and there's a nice piece of topside in the fridge. I thought I'd do you a roast and maybe Yorkshire pudding. Do you like roast potatoes?'

Susannah nodded. 'I love them. That sounds – wonderful.'

Mrs. Minto began taking vegetables out of a basket she had brought with her. They were obviously freshly picked, and Susannah, eager to say the right thing, asked whether Mr. Minto had grown them.

Mrs. Minto looked up from her task and fixed the girl with a reproving stare. 'No, miss. My husband didn't grow these. Mr. Minto's been dead these three years. I'd not be coming here if my Jack was alive. He wouldn't have let me. He didn't hold with – well, with such goings-on!'

Susannah's face suffused with colour and she stared in embarrassment down at her feet. She had heard that country folk were outspoken, but surely Mrs. Minto was going too far.

'Not that it's anything to do with me, you understand.' The housekeeper was putting potatoes into the sink and running water over them. 'I've no doubt I'm old-fashioned. You're not the first couple to think a wedding ring's an unnecessary encumbrance.'

Susannah drew a deep breath. 'Yes – well, some things aren't that simple.'

'Nowadays they're not. Couples setting up house together with nary a scrap of conscience about the babies they bring into the world.'

Susannah turned away. 'If you've got everything you need, Mrs. Minto . . .'

'Now don't you go getting upset over what I say.' Mrs. Minto seemed to be finding a conscience of her own. 'Mind, I wouldn't have thought it of that man – Don Fernando. I liked him. Real gentleman he was when he was here last year. Used to open doors for me, and always said thank you for everything.' She shook her head reminiscently. 'That's why I remembered him. Only came once. Been lots of visitors here since. But I remembered that – his courtesy.'

Susannah turned back. 'I'm so glad you approve of something, Mrs. Minto,' she murmured a little dryly, and the housekeeper looked at her sharply. Then she nodded.

'I know,' she said. 'I'm an interfering old woman. I've heard it before. My daughter says it all the time.'

Susannah shook her head, and with a casual word excused herself. In the living-room she walked to the windows and looked out on the walled garden. She was glad to be away from Mrs. Minto's sharp tongue, but she couldn't help but wonder what the other villagers thought of the Cunninghams and their guests. And how often was this cottage used by other people than themselves?

She sighed. It had been strange hearing Mrs. Minto call Fernando *Don* Fernando, and yet she supposed that was how he was addressed in his own country. She knew so little about him. How did one discover the answers to leading questions without appearing to probe? She shook her head again. No doubt he would tell her all about himself in his own good time. Right now, she was content just to be with him.

She wrapped her arms about herself and shivered in anticipation of the night to come. Not even Mrs. Minto's disapproval could destroy the memory of those few minutes before she arrived when Fernando had demonstrated only too clearly how much he loved and wanted her. To imagine the culmination of that love was an ecstasy too great to contemplate without wanting to throw out her arms and show everyone how happy she was. Giving in to the impulse, she spun lightly round on the spot and then came to an abrupt halt as Fernando came running down the stairs and saw her. His hair was damp from the shower he had just taken and he had changed into a white silk shirt with full sleeves that fastened at his wrist with pearl buttons. His trousers were cream, close-fitting at the hip, revealing the taut muscles of his thighs beneath the fine cloth, flaring towards the ankle above suede boots. Several of the buttons on his shirt were unfastened showing the brown skin of his chest, and she could see a silver medallion glinting amongst the hair. She thought he looked dark and alien, more like a pirate of old than a man who ran a prosperous wine-exporting business.

A curiously guarded look entered his eyes as he saw her and turning away he said: 'A drink, I think. What will you have, Susannah?'

She walked slowly across to join him by a small cabinet and gave an involuntary little shrug. 'I don't know. Sherry, perhaps?'

'Sherry?' He looked sharply at her and she took a step backward at the fierceness of his gaze.

'Is there something wrong with that?' she ventured, in surprise.

He tore his gaze away, shaking his head. 'No. No, of course not. Sherry it shall be.'

She moved away to sit on the couch, puzzling over his change of attitude. Then she inwardly chided herself. She was much too sensitive where he was concerned. No doubt he was a little tired, a little tense – just as she was.

He came to join her carrying their drinks. She noticed he was drinking brandy and that when he sat down he left a liberal amount of leather between them. Frowning, she sipped the sherry and covertly watched him as he stood down his glass to take out one of the cheroots he favoured and light it. When he was inhaling with obvious satisfaction, she said:

'Mrs. Minto is preparing us a traditional English meal – roast beef and Yorkshire pudding. I hope you don't mind.'

Fernando rested his dark head against the back of the couch.

'I am not particularly hungry,' he confessed quietly. '*Tortillas* would perhaps be more appropriate.'

'*Tortillas?* Are they pancakes?'

He tilted his head towards her. 'It is the Spanish form of an omelette, but a little more filling than your English omelettes. Have you never tasted them?'

Susannah bent her head. 'How could I? I've never been to Spain.'

'But the Castanas – do they not eat Spanish food?'

'Occasionally Mrs. Travers, that's the housekeeper, makes a special effort on their behalf, but I usually eat whatever the servants are having.'

'I see,' he nodded.

'You – you don't talk much about Spain, do you?' she tendered, with great temerity.

She couldn't be absolutely certain, but she thought he stiffened. 'You are interested in my country?'

'Naturally I am.'

He shrugged. 'What do you wish to know?'

She sighed. Put like that it sounded so cold and impersonal somehow. Searching for words, she said: 'Tell me about where you live. About Cadiz. There's a certain amount of Moorish influence in that part of Spain, isn't there?'

'There is a certain amount of Moorish influence in the whole of Spain,' he commented dryly. 'But you are right to mention Andalusia.' The way he spoke that word was a caress, and Susannah's senses stirred to the feeling in his voice. 'Nowhere was the Moorish rule so strong and enduring. It is a great irony that their civilization should have been overthrown from within, as it were.'

'What do you mean?'

He leant forward resting his elbows on his knees, looking along at her intently. 'The Moorish ruler fell in love with a Christian girl; but he was already married. He tried to supplant his wife with his new love, but she was a jealous woman. She fled from his palace with her son and raised an army to overthrow her husband. She succeeded, and her son was made king in his stead. But the conflict had weakened the Moorish forces and eventually they had to surrender to the onslaught of Christianity.'

Susannah was fascinated. 'What an intriguing story,' she exclaimed, her eyes wide and innocent.

Fernando studied her intent face and then flung himself back on the couch. 'Yes, is it not?' he conceded tautly. 'One day you may go to Granada – to the Alhambra – and see for yourself exactly what the Moorish ruler lost for love!'

'Granada!' Susannah said the word slowly. 'Such beautiful names, aren't they? Cadiz – Seville – Malaga!' She sighed. 'You must miss it very much.'

He gave her a quick look, and then rose abruptly to his feet. 'Yes, I suppose I should.' He walked to the window, looking out, a frown marring his lean features.

Susannah finished her sherry and put down her glass. She didn't altogether understand his mood, and it troubled her that he seemed withdrawn now and almost morose.

'I have heard it is a very beautiful country,' she volunteered awkwardly. 'Particularly Andalusia.'

He turned, leaning back against the window. 'But like all beautiful things, it has a darker side to its nature,' he said harshly. 'There is cruelty as well as beauty.'

Susannah looked down at her hands. 'I expect there is no more cruelty there than anywhere else. It is an imperfect world.'

He strode across the floor. 'I agree. Nevertheless, I doubt you would speak so tolerantly of the *corrida*.'

'The bullfight?'

'*Si.*' He bent his head. 'It is perhaps a fitting description of the more violent forces in our nature.'

'I know very little about it,' she admitted quietly.

'That is obvious.' His tone was almost disparaging. '*Sin duda*, if you saw a ravaged beast spitting its blood into the sawdust of an arena on some otherwise peaceful Sunday afternoon, you would be as disgusted as many of your compatriots!'

Susannah winced at his descriptive ability. 'Why are you telling me this?' she burst out tremulously. 'What do you expect me to say? Do you want me to despise the ability of your compatriots to delight in blood lust? Do you wish me to feel distaste – *loathing*? To decry all Spaniards because of the behaviour of a minority—'

'They are not a minority. The *corrida* is in our blood. It is a way of life!'

'All right. All right!' Susannah rose to her feet unsteadily, pressing the palms of her hands over her ears. 'I don't want to talk about it any more.' She made a confused movement of her shoulders. 'I don't know what you're trying to do – unless it's to destroy what's between us. If that's what you want to do, you don't have to go to such nauseating lengths—'

He uttered an expletive in his own language and then throwing his half-smoked cheroot into the empty fire grate he came to her, grasping her arms in a savage hold, hauling her close against him. '*Idiota!*' he groaned against her mouth. '*Mi guapa idiota!* Do you not know how I feel – how I despise myself for wanting you so much that I am prepared to go to these lengths to possess you!' His fingers cupped her throat. 'I do not think I am

75

worthy of you, Susannah *mia!*'

Susannah raised her own hands to cover his. 'Don't say such things, Fernando,' she breathed, looking up at him with eyes that revealed all too transparently what her feelings were. 'I agreed to come here, remember?'

He gathered her more closely against him. 'And when the Castanas leave for New York,' he murmured huskily, 'will you be going with them?'

Susannah pressed her face against his chest. 'Do you want me to?'

Fernando lifted her chin. 'Me – I want you to stay in London. But I am selfish. I cannot bear to think of coming to England to find you gone.'

'Oh, Fernando.' She caught her breath. 'I won't go to New York. I don't think I could bear to think of so many thousands of miles between us.'

'Susannah.' His voice was thickening with emotion, and his mouth was devouring hers when a throat was cleared behind them, and Mrs. Minto said:

'Excuse me, I'm sure, but can I lay the table for dinner, sir?'

Fernando closed his eyes for a minute, and then put Susannah away from him and turned to face the unsmiling face of the housekeeper.

'Ah, Señora Minto,' he inclined his head politely. 'I hope you are well, *señora.*'

Mrs. Minto thawed the tiniest bit. 'I'm very well, thank you, Don Fernando.' She indicated the cutlery in her hands. 'Can I set the table?'

'But of course.' Fernando gave her a faint bow, and then bent to extract another cheroot from his case on the table.

Susannah admired his composure. He was completely in control of himself again, no doubt an indication of his breeding, while she was still shaken and trembling, bereft from the enveloping warmth of his nearness.

Mrs. Minto began to lay the polished table in the dining-alcove, taking cut glasses from a sideboard and placing them beside each raffia mat. Fernando lit his cheroot and then after a devastating glance at Susannah, disrupting all her new-found composure, he strolled casually towards the housekeeper, asking her about her married daughter, even remembering her daughter's name. Mrs. Minto blossomed under his attentions like a full-blown rose, and Susannah thought that no one could entirely resist such charm if he chose to exert it.

The meal when it was served was good and wholesome without having much in the way of embellishment. A vegetable broth was followed by the roast beef, with a fruit flan and cream to finish. Unfortunately neither of them did full justice to the food, and Susannah was intensely conscious of the housekeeper's disapproval when she came to remove their plates.

By the time coffee had been served and Mrs. Minto had finished her chores in the kitchen, it was well after nine o'clock. Because they were both aware of the housekeeper's presence, Fernando switched on the television set that resided on one of the broad shelves beside the fireplace, and Susannah tried to concentrate on the film that was showing. It was a terrifying study in fear set in a lonely cottage miles from any other form of civilization, about a young girl who had arranged to meet her lover there, unaware that he was the psychopathic killer who had already murdered half a dozen other women. Susannah was conscious of Fernando's eyes upon her at certain points in the narrative and she smiled without looking at him, realizing he was amusing himself by identifying them with the situation being enacted on the screen.

Mrs. Minto eventually emerged from the kitchen, putting on her coat. 'Well, I'm going now, sir,' she said, addressing herself to Fernando. 'There's nothing else you want, is there?'

Fernando rose to his feet. 'I do not think so, thank you, Señora Minto.' He smiled. 'The dinner was delicious, and I do appreciate the work you have done for us.'

Mrs. Minto looked flustered. 'Why, it was nothing, Don Fernando,' she denied, looking embarrassed when he pressed a note into her hand. 'But – thank you, anyway. I'm sure I hope you and – and the young lady find everything to your liking. Would you like me to come back in the morning and cook breakfast—'

'That will not be necessary, thank you, *señora*.' Fernando was firm. 'Give my regards to your daughter, will you not?'

'That I will.' Mrs. Minto nodded vigorously and moved to the door. 'I'll say good night, then.'

'Good night.' Fernando inclined his head in that gesture which was half bow, half dismissal. Susannah glanced round and bade the housekeeper a brief 'Cheerio,' and then sighed with relief when the door closed behind her. Fernando secured the lock and then walked back to where he had been lounging on the couch, flinging himself down and stretching lazily.

'*Pues?* You do not like her?' he inquired, looking at Susannah out of the corners of his eyes.

Susannah tried not to be distracted by the broad expanse of his brown chest. 'I – I neither like nor dislike her,' she said honestly. 'I – she – we had a difference of opinion earlier.'

'What was that about?' He frowned. 'Ah, let me guess – she did not approve of our being here, *si*? *Ya me lo figuro.*'

Susannah shrugged. 'She has a very high opinion of you, anyway.'

Fernando gave an impatient snort. 'To Señora Minto, there is only *negro y blanco* – black and white. No shades between.'

Susannah smiled. 'I think she considered you beyond such behaviour.'

Fernando closed his eyes. 'Too old, perhaps.'

'You're not old!'

He opened his eyes. 'Compared to you? Oh, yes, I am, Susannah. There are sixteen years between us, remember.'

Susannah pressed her lips together. 'Don't say things like that. Age is not important.'

'At your age, I would agree. But each year means a greater experience of life. I feel – very experienced when I am with you, *pequeña*.'

78

Susannah got up from her armchair and came to sit beside him on the couch, close beside him, sliding her hand across his chest, feeling the heavy beat of his heart. Her fingers encountered the small medallion suspended from its fine silver chain and she lifted it, leaning forward to examine it closely. It was the usual kind of disc made to commemorate one of the numerous saints of the Catholic religion, but on the reverse side there was a small inscription: *Pilar, 1932*. She looked up into his face. 'What does this mean?' she asked curiously.

Fernando looked down at the medallion in her hand. 'It belonged to my mother,' he told her quietly. 'My father gave it to her on the occasion of their marriage. When she died it was given to me.'

'I see.' Susannah fingered the disc. 'Did she – that is – has she been dead very long?'

'Very long,' he conceded, somewhat grimly. 'She died when I was ten years old.'

Susannah looked up at him again. It was hard to imagine the young Fernando, but the vulnerability of such a disaster to any small boy made her lean closer against him and rest her head on his shoulder.

'Did you miss her?' she asked, the compassion evident in her voice.

Fernando seemed to stiffen. 'It was a long time ago. I have forgotten any agony of mind I suffered at that time. An aunt – a sister of my father's – came to live with us, and she took my mother's place quite adequately.'

Susannah frowned. 'That sounds – cold!'

He sighed. 'I suppose it does. But in my country one is not permitted the indulgence of self-pity. My mother was dead – it was an inescapable fact and we had to accept it. My father made the best arrangements he could to prevent any disruption of the household.'

Susannah shook her head, the silky swathe of her hair swinging against his skin. 'And it was so simple to replace your mother?' she exclaimed incredulously.

His arms closed around her, and she felt his lips against her hair. 'No. No, of course it was not,' he admitted emotively. 'And my father would no doubt tell you that my

79

mother's death had a most disagreeable effect upon me. My aunt and I did not – how do you say it – get along? We were not *simpatico, no?* I can remember being in trouble more often than not.'

Susannah nestled closer. 'That sounds more human.'

'*Si.* I was very human.' His tone was dry. 'When I was your age my father despaired of ever being able to—' He broke off suddenly and drew a deep breath. 'But that is enough. You do not wish to hear of my disreputable past.'

'Oh, but I do!' She sat up. 'I – I want to know everything about you.'

Fernando looked into her flushed face and then shook his head, his eyes half closed. 'I am tired,' he said softly. 'Are you?'

Susannah shivered. 'A – a little.'

'Then I suggest we go to bed, *si?*' He pressed a light kiss to her parted lips. 'You go up. I will smoke a cheroot and follow in five minutes.'

Susannah nodded. The moment had come and there was no drawing back now. The pleasant evening they had spent, the homely aromas of the food they had consumed, the television still playing away uselessly in the corner were suddenly a sensitized sequence of events that flashed before her eyes. She went up the stairs automatically without looking back. She washed, cleaned her teeth, and got undressed, putting on the white lawn nightgown she had bought several months ago and never worn. Then she climbed into the enormous bed, aware that she had never slept between silk sheets before, and turned out the light.

Lying there in the darkness she heard Fernando come up the stairs and then the sound of running water in the bathroom. He had obviously entered from the landing and she tensed into a stiff imitation of herself. It was no good. She was frightened. And she didn't know what to do about it.

The bathroom light went out and the door to the bedroom opened. In the gloom she could vaguely make out his shadowy form as he moved towards the bed. But he didn't immediately get into bed. He sat down at her side and she could feel his intent dark eyes searching for hers.

'Why did you turn the light out?' he asked gently.

Susannah found it difficult to articulate between chattering teeth. 'I – I – I didn't know you – you wanted – it on.'

He sighed. 'What's wrong? You sound positively petrified. I did not know I was such a terrifying individual.'

'You – you're – n – not.'

Fernando shook his head. 'That is a relief,' he commented with some irony. He slid his fingers to her throat, smoothing his thumbs over her ears, causing a little of the tension to leave her. He drew back the bedcovers to her waist and even in the gloom the whiteness of her gown was clearly visible. '*Que?*' he murmured questioningly. 'You are wearing a nightgown?'

She nodded jerkily, stretching out her arms to him stiffly, touching only the firm warm skin of his body. Fernando seemed to hesitate a moment and then he caught both her hands in his and said a trifle grimly, 'Susannah! Something you said! Something about never having – done this sort of thing before. *Madre de dios*, did you mean it?'

She nodded again, clenching her teeth to stop their chattering.

'*Cristo!*'

With a violent gesture he dropped her hands and rose to his feet, turning away from her and walking to the foot of the bed. He opened his suitcase, rummaged inside it, and came out with a kind of white bathrobe which he swiftly donned to cover his nakedness. Then he walked to the light and switched it on, deliberately dispelling any intimacy between them.

'Why did you not make it plain?' he demanded harshly. '*Dios*, would you add the defilement of an innocent to my other sins?'

Susannah was mortified. 'Fernando, please – what have I done?' She caught her breath on a sob. 'Don't you want me any more?'

81

Fernando closed his eyes and then opened them again. 'You are talking like an *idiota!*' he snapped savagely, striding about the room before coming to a halt at the foot of the bed. 'Why did you not tell me this evening?'

Susannah struggled into a sitting position. 'But I told you yesterday, Fernando,' she protested tearfully.

He stood breathing heavily. 'Women say these things. They do not mean them. They simply wish the man to believe that he is the first—'

'But you are!'

'*Por dios*, I know that.' He turned away as though he could not bear to look at her. 'What a fool I have been!'

Susannah stared at his broad back helplessly. Then she slid out of bed and padded on bare feet to his side. 'Fernando,' she pleaded, 'don't be angry with me! I – I couldn't bear that.'

He turned slowly and looked down at her, the heavy swathe of pale hair combined with her demure lawn gown giving her an almost childlike appearance. '*Basta*, Susannah!' he muttered thickly. 'Go to bed! I will sleep in the other room. You need have no fear of me!'

'*Fernando!*' She stared up at him appealingly, but he could stand no more. With a grim determination, he put her aside and strode out of the room, slamming the door behind him.

She cried for a long time, her face buried under the covers so that he would not hear her; but then she must have slept, because she was dreaming, a terrible, terrifying dream where Fernando became the monster of the film they had watched that evening, the maniacal killer of half a dozen women. She was trapped in the cottage with him and he was searching for her. She hid in every imaginable place, but he always found her, always kept coming after her. But then when he cornered her and she wanted him to kill her, he wouldn't do it. He stepped away from her and she began to cry, and cry and cry . . .

'*Susannah!* Susannah *mia*, what is it? Susannah, wake up, wake up! No one's going to hurt you!'

She blinked rapidly, looking up into Fernando's concerned eyes. Someone had put on the bedside lamp and he was sitting on the side of the bed in his bathrobe, his hair tumbled from the pillow.

'Fernando?' she breathed slowly, taking great gulping breaths of air, becoming aware of the dampness of her cheeks. She scrubbed a hand across her eyes. 'Wh – what time is it?'

Fernando glanced at his wrist watch. 'It's a little after one o'clock,' he told her gently. 'You've been dreaming. You were crying ...'

Susannah began to nod as the terrible remembrance of the nightmare came back to her. 'It – it was awful!' she choked, her breath coming in shallow gulps. 'It – it was the film—'

Fernando frowned. 'Ah, the remote cottage – the killer of so many women!' He nodded. 'I understand.' He rose to his feet.

'Wh – where are you going?' she cried, jerking upright, reaching for his hand, the hand that a moment ago had been smoothing her brow.

Fernando's frown deepened. 'You are all right now. I will go back to my room—'

'*No!* Oh, no, please – don't!' Her voice was urgent, her eyes wide and alarmed.

'I must!' His voice was harsh – as before.

She began to cry again, deep racking sobs that shook her slender form, and her hair fell in a curtain about her face buried in her hands.

Fernando watched her for a long agonizing period and then with a muffled exclamation, he said' '*A fondo*, I will stay. But that is all – do you understand?'

She raised a tear-wet face to his, and nodded silently. He went and turned out the light and walked round the bed, sliding on it beside her. He did not take off his robe, nor did he get beneath the bedcovers, and she had the sense to understand why. All the same, some time before morning she found herself snuggled into the small of his back, her arm encircling his waist trapped in the folds of his bathrobe ...

CHAPTER SIX

Susannah awoke to an unusual feeling of apprehension and could not understand why. The sun was shining, and the yellow curtains at the windows were filling the room with a golden light. She blinked, not immediately identifying her surroundings, but then sat up with a start as she recalled the humiliating events of the night before. Her eyes turned swiftly to the bed beside her, but Fernando had gone, only the imprint of his head on the pillow bearing witness to the fact that he had stayed with her last night.

Haste, panic-stricken haste, brought her out of bed on the instant. She searched impatiently for her silk dressing gown and putting it on hurried to the door. But she stopped suddenly and did a double take. Something which she had noticed but which had not at once made any impression now focused her attention. Fernando's suitcase was no longer on the ottoman beside hers.

Quickening her step she opened the bedroom door and came out on to the landing. There was no sound from anywhere and she opened the door of the second bedroom with trembling fingers, not really surprised when she found it empty. Then she went downstairs.

Again, there was no sign of Fernando, but propped on the low coffee table in a position where she could not fail to see it was a note. An awful sinking feeling assailed her as she approached that note, and she picked it up reluctantly, half guessing what it would say.

Mi amada,

I cannot take back the past. I can only hope you will not think too unkindly of me in the future. I cannot say that I regret this time we have spent together. It is a memory I will always treasure. But you are a beautiful young woman, Susannah, and one day you will meet a young man who is worthy of your love and forget all

*about me. Please believe that I love you, and that it is
because I love you that I am not prepared to create a
relationship between us that must be doomed from the
start. I am too old for you. I have seen too much of life
not to know I am right. I have arranged for a cab to
collect you at eleven o'clock to take you back to
London. I shall be gone by then.*

Forgive me, Fernando.

Susannah read the note twice and then sank down on
to the couch and stared blindly into the empty fire-grate.
He had gone, really gone. He had left the cottage, goodness knows how long ago, and was probably aboard his
plane by now. Had he had this all planned? Was this night
to be their only time together? Had he already arranged
his departure before he left for the country? He made no
mention of seeing her again, not even on his next trip to
London, and in any case he knew she was leaving the
Castanas, so how would he find her even if he wanted
to . . .?

Eventually she dragged herself into the kitchen and
made herself some coffee. She had to do something to
arouse herself from the extreme state of apathy into
which she had sunk. Somehow she had to pull herself
together sufficiently to wash and dress and pack her
things, and be ready to leave when the taxi came at
eleven o'clock.

As there was no sign of a key and the cottage door had
a Yale lock Susannah slammed it as she came out and
climbed into the cab without looking back. If the driver
thought it strange that his fare should be a rather wan-
faced girl who had apparently been spending the week-
end alone at the cottage he kept his thoughts to himself
and chatted away about how mild the weather was for
the time of year and wasn't it a shame that some football
club had lost their match against a European side?

By the time they reached London it was long after
lunch, but when Susannah alighted at the Castana house
and tried to pay her fare she was informed that it had
already been taken care of. She entered the house with an

85

intense feeling of desolation and started when Mrs. Travers appeared from the kitchen.

'You're back early, miss,' she exclaimed. 'I thought you were to be away until this evening.'

'I was.' Susannah sighed. 'Are Señor and Señora Castana at home?'

'No, miss, they're out. An old friend of theirs, a Señora d'Alvarez, arrived yesterday afternoon, and I believe they've taken her to visit mutual friends.'

'I see.' Susannah felt relieved.

Mrs. Travers clicked her tongue. 'Is something wrong, miss? You're looking awfully peaky. Oh, I suppose you're hungry.' She paused. 'Well, I was just leaving for my sister's, but if you're hungry—'

Susannah shook her head. 'No, really, Mrs. Travers. It's quite all right. I – I didn't come back to upset your afternoon. You go ahead. In any case, I – I may be going out again.'

The idea had just occurred to her. Margaret, she thought, like a drowning man clutching at straws, that was where she would go. To see Margaret and Peter and baby Toni. It would be so good to be with people who cared what happened to her . . .

'You mean – you slept with him? Oh, Susannah!' Margaret French stared at her friend with anxious eyes. 'Whatever possessed you to agree to such a thing?'

The two girls were talking in the kitchen of Margaret and Peter's modern semi on a large housing estate at Kennington. Peter was in the living-room entertaining Toni, tactfully keeping out of the way. Margaret had insisted on making Susannah an omelette, which she had managed to eat half of, and now they were sharing a pot of coffee.

Susannah traced the pattern of the formica on the kitchen table with her forefinger. 'I've told you, Margaret. Nothing happened.'

'I know. But – well, if this Fernando hadn't been a decent sort of man it could have.'

'I know that.'

86

'So – whatever were you thinking of? Heavens, you've only known the man two weeks!'

'He was leaving for Spain tomorrow. This was his last week-end in England.'

'So?'

'So I love him, Margaret.' Susannah had to press her lips together to stop them from trembling.

'But you know nothing about him! You don't even have his address.'

'I – I could get it.'

'Where from? The Castanas? Would they give it to you?'

'I don't know.' Susannah hunched her shoulders. 'Oh, Margaret, haven't you ever felt like doing anything crazy? Has there never been a man in your life who hasn't conformed to – to – certain conventialities?'

'We're not talking about me,' observed Margaret dryly. 'Susannah – after all you've said about your mother!'

'I know, I know.'

Margaret shook her head and rose to her feet carrying her empty coffee cup to the sink. 'What you need is a steady boy-friend, someone who'd knock all these wild ideas out of your head,' she said firmly. 'If you were married you wouldn't have time for – for day-dreaming!'

'I wouldn't call it that.'

'Well, what would you call it? Susannah, you're not a child. You know perfectly well that some men – when they're away from home – are just ripe for an illicit affair—'

'Fernando isn't like that!' declared Susannah unsteadily.

'How do you know? What do you know about him? He could be married for all you know!'

Susannah felt sick. 'He's not. I know he's not.'

'How? Did he tell you so?'

'No.'

'And he would hardly tell you if he was married, would he?'

'Oh, Margaret—'

87

'I'm only trying to be practical, Susannah. If he loves you as you say he does, why has he gone? Why hasn't he arranged to see you again?'

'He – he thinks he's too old for me.'

'Oh, really? And when did age stop any man from getting what he wanted?'

'That's not a fair analogy.'

'I know. But honestly, Sue, do you really think that's all that's stopping him?'

'I don't know. He – he comes from a very old Spanish family. Perhaps they would oppose any involvement between him and an English girl.'

'I see. So now it's his family who are the villains. He's not a boy, you know, Sue! You said he's forty. Don't you think it's entirely plausible that he's married at that age?'

'Oh, stop it, stop it!' Susannah covered her ears with her hands. 'He loves me, I know he does!'

Margaret's eyes warmed with compassion and she came back and pressed Susannah's shoulder. 'Perhaps he does at that,' she commented wryly. 'Why else didn't he take what you so consummately offered?'

Susannah was trembling, tears hovering on the brink of her eyes. 'That's what I keep asking myself,' she admitted chokingly.

Margaret sighed and went to sit opposite her again. 'All right. Suppose we accept that he does love you. What then? What are you going to do? Go to the States with the Castanas?'

Susannah shook her head. 'I – I couldn't do that.'

Margaret nodded. 'Well, I suppose I can understand that,' she conceded. 'So – you need another job.'

'Yes.'

'Then why don't you come out of private tutoring and get yourself a job in a school—'

'—where I'll meet some suitable young men,' Susannah finished for her.

'Well, why not? Susannah, do you want to remain a spinster all your life?'

Susannah wiped her eyes, amusement twitching at her

lips. 'That's a rather old-fashioned word, isn't it? Nowadays people say bachelor girls.'

'All right. Do you want to stay single all your life? Don't you want a home – a family?'

'Of course I do. But I don't just want to get married simply as an alternative to staying single. I want to marry the man I love.'

'Fernando.'

'Yes.'

Margaret shook her head. 'So you'll take another private post?'

'I suppose so. I – I haven't given the matter a lot of thought.'

'You haven't had much time,' pointed out Margaret dryly.

'No.' Susannah finished her coffee. 'But I must tell Señor Castana that I shan't be going to New York, though. He asked me to give him as much time as possible to find a replacement. He wants an English governess for Eduardo.'

Margaret nodded. 'Well, you know you can always stay with us if you haven't found anything before the Castanas leave. We have loads of room and we'd love to have you, you know that.'

Susannah was sorry when the time came to leave the Frenches. For a few hours she had known the relaxation of a real home and she was loath to exchange it for the solitary isolation of her apartment at the Castana house. Perhaps there was something to be said for being married, she thought dejectedly, as Peter drove her back to Lorrimer Terrace. At least she would have a home of her own that way.

The next morning she encountered the Castanas' house guest for the first time. Lucie Castana brought her to the schoolroom while Susannah was giving Eduardo his lessons and introduced her as Señora Monica d'Alvarez.

To her surprise, Susannah found that Monica d'Alvarez was an American. She had, she said, lived in Spain for a great number of years, but her accent remained as strident as ever. Although Susannah estimated her age to be nearing fifty, Monica dressed in the manner of a much younger woman. Obviously, she did not favour the greys and blacks that one read were much favoured by older Latin matrons, and instead she was wearing a rather garishly-patterned tunic top over scarlet lounging pants. Her hair was bleached to a silvery whiteness that contrasted sharply with her rather sallow complexion, and from the amount of nicotine staining her bony fingers Susannah thought she must smoke almost incessantly. And yet, for all that, she was not an unattractive woman, with a dry sense of humour that was lost on Lucie Castana.

She showed a genuine interest in what Eduardo was doing, asking Susannah pertinent questions, praising the boy for being able to read English so well.

'An English governess is always best,' remarked Lucie complacently, paying Susannah a somewhat indirect compliment. 'Carlos would employ no other.'

Monica d'Alvarez raised her narrow plucked eyebrows. 'We Americans get along,' she commented dryly. Then to Susannah: 'Are you looking forward to going to the States? It's a great country. You'll have a hell of a time! The men aren't blind over there like they are where I come from.'

'Spanish men are not blind, Monica,' said Lucie shortly. 'We have a deeper respect for convention, that is all.'

Monica grimaced, and Susannah felt an unwilling smile touching her lips. 'Yeah? Well, you call it what you like, honey. But I'm telling you – in the States you don't have to lead a horse to water and then show it how to drink as well!'

Lucie's lips curled at Monica's rather coarse metaphor, and Susannah thought it was a suitable moment to tell her that she would not be going to New York with them.

'What?' Lucie looked horrified. 'But why not?'

Susannah bit her lower lip. 'I'd rather get another post over here, *señora*.'

Lucie seethed, 'Does my husband know this?'

'Not yet, *señora*. I intended telling him today, but as you were talking about it . . .'

'I see.' Lucie tapped her palms together impatiently. 'You realize that we will have to find someone else immediately and that when we do you will be redundant, do you not?'

'Yes, *señora*.' Susannah looked reluctantly towards Eduardo. Surely Lucie was not going to make a confrontation out of this.

But now the older woman, Monica d'Alvarez, was looking interested. 'What do you mean about taking another post over here?' she asked. 'In England, do you mean, or does the continent appeal to you?'

Susannah shrugged. 'I will have to see what I am offered, *señora*.'

Monica nodded. 'Sure. Sure you will. Well, I'd be willing to take you on.'

Susannah didn't know who looked the most shocked, herself or Lucie Castana.

'You would!' exclaimed Lucie impatiently. 'Why would you require the services of a governess? Marla is fourteen years of age. She goes to the convent school, does she not?'

Monica d'Alvarez brought out a pack of long American cigarettes and put one between her lips. Lighting it, she said: 'Sure. Marla goes to the convent, but I'm not so mad about that idea. Hell, she's as much an American as she is a Spaniard. She speaks English as well as I do. Why shouldn't she take English lessons instead of Spanish ones?'

Lucie's nostrils flared. 'The convent is an excellent establishment. I was educated there myself.'

Monica's lips twisted. 'Okay, don't get hot under the collar. I'm not cribbing the convent. I'm only saying that Marla might be offered a choice.'

Lucie's fingers tapped together restlessly. 'Your husband would never agree, Monica.'

'Maybe not.' Monica shrugged. 'Maybe I won't ask him.' She turned to Susannah. 'Well, honey? What do you say? How does the idea appeal to you? It's your decision, after all.'

Susannah had been standing listening to their conversation while a wave of consternation swept over her. Monica d'Alvarez was married to a Spaniard, a small voice inside her was saying; she lived in Spain, and after Lucie's appraisal of the convent school it must be somewhere near where the Castanas themselves used to live. Fernando was a friend of the Castanas. He must live in that area, too.

'I – I don't know—' she began helplessly, half afraid to consider what this might mean.

'It is a totally different way of life,' put in Lucie coldly. 'I do not think you would like it, *señorita.*'

'Hey, don't put her off!' Monica frowned impatiently at the Spanish woman. 'Just because you can't have her, it doesn't mean that we shouldn't.'

Susannah had to say something. 'I – you live in Spain, *señora?*'

'That's right. In a little place called Alvaridad. Actually,' Monica pulled a face, 'it's called for my husband's family. The Alvarez vineyards are famous the world over.'

Susannah licked her dry lips. 'Is that – the southern part of Spain, *señora?*'

'Yeah! Andalucia!' The way Monica said it it had no magic whatsoever. 'We're pretty near Cadiz, and not too far from Seville. The place is steeped in history.'

Susannah swallowed a sense of panic that rose into her throat. Andalucia was not such a vast area that she might not be able to discover exactly where the Cuevas family had their vineyards. But did she want to know? Could she go to Spain knowing that she might meet Fernando again? After all, he had not asked her to do so, had not even wanted to see her again. And yet he had said he loved her . . .

'It – it sounds intriguing,' she admitted, not wanting to commit herself.

Monica was delighted. 'You think so?'

Lucie looked disdainfully at them both. 'Señorita

King may find she has little to do in her spare time,' she remarked.

Monica frowned. 'Well, I guess I have to tell you that there isn't much in the way of entertainment at that. We live a pretty ordinary existence most of the time.' She shrugged. 'Of course, it depends what you like doing. The weather's pretty good mostly, and we're not too far from the coast.'

'Señorita King will miss her friends,' Lucie pointed out.

Monica gave the other woman a killing look. 'What do you say, Miss King?' she asked encouragingly, turning to Susannah.

'Do not rush her,' snapped Lucie, making her own dissatisfaction at this turn of events abundantly clear. 'We cannot all come to these sudden decisions, Monica.'

'What's to decide?' Monica drew on her cigarette deeply. 'Either she wants to come or she doesn't.'

Susannah didn't know what to say. 'You say your daughter is – fourteen, *señora*?'

'That's right.'

'And she is your only child?'

'She is.' Monica gave a resigned gesture. 'You'll have no trouble with her. Spanish girls are brought up to be boringly obedient.' She ignored the way Lucie bristled at this. 'That's why I want you to teach her. I want her to realize that she has a mind of her own.'

Lucie sniffed. 'Girls from good families have breeding, Monica. That is something you know perhaps very little about.'

Monica turned on her. 'Oh, yeah? Heck, Lucie, stop trying so hard to make the girl change her mind.'

'I didn't know she had already decided.'

'Perhaps she hasn't at that. And if you have your way she never will.'

'Marla is better off at the convent,' said Lucie adamantly.

'Oh, is she?' Monica nodded. 'And what will be ahead of her after that? Engagement – marriage to some chosen suitor? Oh, no, not for Marla. Do you think I want her to

93

turn out like me? Like you? Frustrated to the point of boredom. Married to men who scarcely know of our existence? Come off it, Lucie! You know I'm right. You don't love Carlos. You never did. You wouldn't keep making a play for Fernando if you really loved your husband!'

Fernando!

Susannah caught her breath. Monica had used his name. And it had to be the same Fernando, for hadn't she seen the way Lucie looked at him? That meant that Monica knew him too!

'Monica! *Por favor!*'

Clearly Monica had gone too far now and Lucie glared angrily at her, her flashing eyes indicative of her feelings. Monica sighed and shook her head.

'Okay, okay, I'll shut up! But it's the truth and you know it.' She turned once more to Susannah. 'Well, honey? How long do you need to think it over?'

Susannah was trying to make up her mind. Of course, there was always the possibility that Monica d'Alvarez would forget all about this conversation as soon as she left the room. Did she want that? Or was she prepared to go to Spain and risk seeing Fernando again?

The maid's knock interrupted them. 'Excuse me, Señora Castana,' she said politely, 'but there's a gentleman downstairs asking for Señora d'Alvarez.'

Monica swung round. 'Did he give his name?'

'Yes, madam. A Mr. Rosenberg—'

'*Max!* It's Max!' Monica's face glowed with animation. 'Lucie, did you hear that? Max is here! Oh, how wonderful!'

She went quickly to the door and Susannah's shoulders sagged. No doubt now she would forget all about the idea of employing a governess. And perhaps it was just as well at that. Although . . .

'Just a minute.' Monica was turning. 'I'll be back later to hear what you have to say, honey. If it's money you're worried about, don't be. I'll double whatever Lucie's paying you, and throw in a month's salary in advance as an assurance of good faith.'

Susannah clenched her fists, and then took an impulsive step forward. 'There – there's no need for you to come back,' she faltered, as Monica paused expectantly. 'That is – not to hear my decision. I – I will come and be Marla's governess, if you're sure you want me.'

CHAPTER SEVEN

SUSANNAH had arrived in Madrid in the heat of the day when even the airport officials showed a distinct lack of enthusiasm for their duties, and had flown on to Seville while Spain drowsed in the *siesta* hours. After the magnificence of the Pyrenees which even now were still clothed in the snows of winter it was a dramatic contrast to land on tarmac made soft by the heat of the sun. But it was a contrast wholly to her liking. Even so, the air-conditioning of the aircraft had not prepared her for the onslaught of heat which hit her as she left the plane, or for the dazzling effect of white-painted buildings on the naked eye. However, by the time she had negotiated the formalities at Seville the cooler draught of evening was freshening the air and lengthening the shadows, and only the discomfiting warmth of the cream slack suit she had worn to travel in reminded her of the striking change of temperature.

Emerging into the reception area she looked about her expectantly. She marshalled her two suitcases and breathed a sigh of relief. Now that she was here it hardly seemed possible that it was only hours since she had left the Frenches' house in Kennington. The past two months had been so hectic, and she was glad that they were over at last. She had had so many things to contend with – not least her own conscience.

Of course, once she knew Susannah was leaving, Lucie Castana had made things as unpleasant for her as possible, and not till her husband had found a satisfactory replacement did she refrain from criticizing the girl at every opportunity. Naturally, Monica d'Alvarez had had to return to Spain, but she had kept in touch with Susannah and made the eventual arrangements for her journey. Susannah could have done with the American woman's support at this time. She had liked her, even though she had found her conversation a little coarse at times, but Lucie had lost no time in telling her that Monica was notorious for her unconventionality, and that she had had dozens of affairs. This man in London, Max Rosenberg, was only one of many lovers she had had, and if Susannah imagined she would have an easier time with the Alvarez family she was very much mistaken.

Susannah had tried to ignore what she had been told. Señora d'Alvarez's personal involvements did not concern her. It was true that she and Max Rosenberg had seen a lot of one another while she was in London, and that on the rare occasions when Susannah had seen them together their attitude towards one another had been disturbingly intimate, but that was nothing to do with her. Besides, she had enough problems of her own with Margaret.

Her friend had made it plain that she considered her behaviour in accepting this post as reckless in the extreme, and in the few days that Susannah had spent with the Frenches, prior to leaving for Spain, Margaret had done her utmost to persuade her to change her mind and find another post here in England.

But Susannah had been unable to draw back. Maybe she was behaving recklessly, but if she gave up now she might spend the rest of her life wondering why Fernando had left so abruptly. Perhaps he had reasons for keeping his life in England apart from his life in Spain, perhaps he was married as Margaret had suggested, but if she never made the effort to find out she could never be sure. She refused to consider what she might do if he should prove to be married . . .

The reception area which had been quite crowded when she first arrived had now quietened and she was beginning to wonder when she was to be met and who was to meet her when a polite, but alien, voice inquired: 'Señorita King, *por favor*?'

Susannah turned to confront the man who had spoken. He was about her own height and very slim, with the swarthy cast of his race. He was dressed in the discreet uniform of a chauffeur, and she couldn't help but wonder how he could appear so cool. 'Yes,' she answered now, 'I am Susannah King. Who are you?'

The man drew himself up to his full height and she would not have been surprised if he had clicked his heels. 'Pedro Morales, *señorita. El chofer de* Don Fernando Ramirez Esteban Cuevas d'Alvarez, *a su disposicion!*'

Susannah's fingers twisted the strap of her handbag. 'I – I see,' she managed with difficulty, but two names had registered out of that stream of Spanish – Fernando and Cuevas! What did it mean? That they were common names in this country? Or that this man – this chauffeur – was in the employ of Fernando? Shaking her head, she forced herself to go on: 'How – how do you do? Do you speak English?'

The chauffeur bent to pick up her cases. 'A little, *señorita*,' he conceded slowly. 'Come – *por favor.*'

Outside the airport buildings the fierceness of the sun had abated and Susannah breathed deeply as she followed him across the parking area to where a low-slung black limousine was waiting. As he stowed her suitcases in the boot she studied the coat of arms on the door. It was the crest of the Alvarez family, incorporating an eagle and a pomegranate, and unaccountably she shivered. What did it all mean? Was Fernando a relative of the Alvarez family? She was confused and vaguely apprehensive.

Because of his evident difficulties with her language and her limited knowledge of Spanish, they spoke little on the journey to the Alvarez estate. Susannah wished she could have questioned him about the family, but perhaps it was as well that she could not. She was only a governess here after all, an employee as Pedro Morales was an employee, and she doubted very much whether he would have been prepared to discuss his employers with her.

To her disappointment their route did not take them into Seville itself, but instead they turned south on to the main highway which, had it not been for the fact that they were driving on the right-hand side of the road, might have been a motorway in England. Night was falling and all she could see was the black road ahead and the brilliant illumination of passing headlamps.

Eventually they turned off the motorway to follow a much narrower, winding road, the surface of which was vastly inferior to what she had been used to. She wasn't sure, but she thought that vineyards lined the road, and there was a distinct smell of lemon trees from an orchard hidden behind a high stone wall. She guessed there were houses too, concealed by other walls in the Moorish fashion, and wished it was still daylight. There was so much she wanted to see.

Presently they turned between stone gateposts which in the brief illumination of the headlamps revealed that they were topped by stone eagles, realistically poised for the kill. They left the narrow road to ascend a steep gradient between trees that pressed in on all sides. She guessed they had reached the Alvarez estate and that this was the drive which led up to the house. Her nerves tensed and on impulse she leant forward to the driver and said: 'Are we almost there? Is this the Alvarez estate?'

Pedro Morales glanced at her over his shoulder. '*Sí, señorita*.' He spread an encompassing hand. 'All estate – *de* Don Fernando.'

Susannah sank back. 'Thank you.' She looked helplessly through the windows. *Don Fernando!* Who was Don Fernando? This man's employer, certainly, but what else? And what had he to do with Monica d'Alvarez?

The car was slowing to a halt and for a moment her heart pounded. But then she saw ahead of them a high stone wall with wrought iron gates closed against them. Pedro sounded his horn and immediately a man came running to unlock the gates and throw them wide, looking curiously into the shadowy interior of the car as it passed.

But Susannah was too intent on her surroundings to pay any attention to the gatekeeper. The car was sweeping to a halt before shallow stone steps leading up to a lamplit patio. Beyond the patio lay the house which even in shadow could be seen to be enormous. An arched entrance led through to an inner courtyard which Susannah could see was illuminated by Moorish lamps hung from a surrounding balcony. There were fountains in the inner

99

courtyard and the sound of their playing was like music on the air.

Pedro Morales got out and came round to assist her and Susannah had to rouse herself with difficulty. But there was so much to see and absorb – palm trees casting pools of shadow, masses of flowers, their colours muted by the amber light from the lamps, urns that spilled flowering shrubs over the shallow steps and twined about the pillars that supported the patio. The building was two-storied, and there were shutters to all the windows, thrown back now so that huge moths fought to gain entrance through the panes of glass lit from within.

Susannah stood on the stone steps waiting for Pedro to retrieve her luggage feeling more apprehensive than ever. Perhaps Lucie Castana had been right, after all. This would be an entirely different way of life. Who could live in magnificent surroundings like these without being affected by them?

Before Pedro had closed the boot of the opulent limousine a black-clad figure came walking through the archway from the inner courtyard. Susannah glanced at the figure nervously, imagining it to be a manservant come to show her to her room. But whoever it was he halted in the shadows and while he could see her very well, she could only vaguely see him.

Her nerves were jumping. The journey, this imposing house, the unseen watcher in the shadows, the darkness – all served to make her uneasy. She turned back to Pedro, silently urging him to hurry. The boot was closed and Pedro picked up her cases, and Susannah breathed a sigh of relief. But when she looked round the black-clad figure had gone, he had disappeared as noiselessly as he had come. She blinked incredulously. She couldn't have imagined it, could she? Surely her nerves were not as torn as that.

'Come!'

Pedro was smiling encouragingly and with a shrug she accompanied him up the shallow steps and across the mosaic tiling of the patio. They entered the inner courtyard through the arched way and Susannah couldn't suppress the shiver that engulfed her as they passed the spot where the figure had been standing.

She was given little time to admire the lamplit court-yard with its wrought iron balconies and hanging plants before a woman dressed all in black apart from a long white apron appeared and approached them. She was the epitome of the Spanish housekeeper with greying hair secured in a knot at the nape of her neck, a sallow skin, and bright inquisitive eyes. She gave Susannah a quick appraising stare and then spoke to Pedro in rapid Spanish. The chauffeur answered equally swiftly and then urged Susannah forward.

'*Este* Señora Gomez, *señorita.*'

Susannah forced a smile, but the woman ignored it. 'You are Señorita King, are you not?' she queried, and at Susannah's nod, she went on: 'I am the housekeeper of Don Fernando's house. If you will come with me, I will show you your room.'

Susannah cast a helpless look in Pedro's direction and chanced a grimace. His conspiratorial grin in return made her feel heaps better suddenly, and she followed the housekeeper with an eager step, aware of Pedro coming behind with her suitcases.

They entered the building through long panelled doors which gave on to an immense hall. The floor was composed of marble tiles in amber and white, while the high arched ceiling was richly panelled and carved with strange-looking figures. The staircase to the upper floor was marble, too, but the balustrade was intricately curled wrought iron. There were statues of saints in the narrow window embrasures, and urns of exotically coloured flowers stood on tall pedestals. It was totally unreal, and Susannah marvelled again that anyone could actually live in such surroundings.

To the left and right of the hall, corridors led away to the farthest reaches of the house. The building was built round the central courtyard, and it was the focal point. The housekeeper did not approach the magnificent staircase as Susannah had half expected, but instead led the way along the right-hand corridor. A great number of doors opened on to this corridor, most of which were closed, but just occasionally Susannah caught a glimpse of the beautifully furnished apartments within.

At the end of the corridor was another staircase, narrow and winding, and this the housekeeper did ascend, glancing round momentarily to assure herself that Susannah was following.

'This is the staircase you will use to reach your room, *señorita*,' she said, with deliberate emphasis, Susannah thought. 'Of course, when you are with the Señorita Marla, you may be permitted to use the other.'

'Yes, *señora*,' Susannah nodded, and was relieved when they emerged on to the upper landing. To her surprise, she saw that they were now on the balcony at the far side of the courtyard, but even as she moved to look over the balcony rail, Señora Gomez threw open the door of a room behind her, and said:

'This is your apartment, *señorita*. As you will see, there is a bathroom – here!'

Susannah turned and stepped into the room as Señora Gomez switched on the lamps. Then she gave an involuntary gasp of pleasure. It was totally unlike the rather drab accommodation she had occupied at the Castana house. Colour-washed walls in apple green, wrought iron tracery behind a wide bed covered with an apricot spread, long wild silk curtains also in apricot, dark wood furniture that in no way dispelled the room's airy lightness.

'It's – beautiful!' she exclaimed.

'I am glad you are satisfied, *señorita*,' observed Señora Gomez calmly, but even she could not entirely hide her gratification at Susannah's enthusiasm. She stood aside for Pedro to deposit the suitcases in the middle of the floor and then after he had left them, she said: 'If you would like a few minutes to wash and tidy yourself, *señorita*, before meeting the *señora*, I will leave you. I will send someone to escort you to the *señora*'s rooms when you are ready.'

Susannah's excitement evaporated as quickly as it had come. The *señora*! And who was that? Monica d'Alvarez? It had to be, didn't it? But how could she inquire anything of this formal housekeeper any more than she could have inquired of Pedro?

Breathing a deep sigh, she nodded. 'I – I would like to change.'

'Very well, *señorita*.' The housekeeper moved towards the door. 'Your meals will be served in your room while you are here,' she added. 'Dinner this evening will be served at nine o'clock.'

Susannah realized as the woman spoke that it was hours since lunch and yet the thought of food had not occurred to her.

'If you would like some coffee, I will have some sent up to you,' the housekeeper was saying now, and Susannah thought how welcome a cup of coffee would be.

'If it's not too much trouble,' she murmured quietly.

Señora Gomez inclined her head. 'Very well. If you will excuse me . . .'

After she had gone, Susannah explored her domain more thoroughly. The adjoining bathroom was as impressive as the bedroom, with an apple green step-in bath that would have accommodated half a dozen people. The taps were beaten gold, the shower curtains apricot, and a generous assortment of bath oils and lotions lined the mirrored shelves.

Stripping off her clothes, she took a shower, revelling in the coolness of the water against her warm and sticky skin. Then she quickly opened one of her suitcases and was fastening the zip of a simple navy day dress when there was a knock at her balcony door. A young maid entered at her summons carrying a tray of coffee, very dark and very Spanish, her inquisitive eyes missing little in that first appraisal.

'*Buenas tardes, señorita*,' she greeted Susannah, with a smile and a little bob. 'Senora Gomez said you wished *cafe*.'

'Thank you.' Susannah secured her zip and straightened. 'Will you put it down on the table? Who are you?'

'Maria, *señorita*.' She put down the tray on the bedside table Susannah had indicated. 'Señora Gomez said to wait and take you to Señora d'Alvarez, *si*?'

Susannah walked over to the tray and poured herself a cup of the aromatic beverage. It tasted as delicious as it smelled, but she looked up in surprise when Maria walked to the door.

'Where are you going?'

'I will wait outside, *señorita*.'

'No – that is – well, that's not necessary, Maria. I – I shan't be a minute.'

Susannah snatched up her brush and began tugging it through the thickness of her hair. She was trying desperately to think of a way to ask Maria about the family, but it wasn't easy.

'Have – have you worked for the Alvarez family for long, Maria?' she asked at last.

Maria shrugged. 'Since I was at school, *señorita*.'

'I see.' Susannah put down the hairbrush and picked up a colourless lipstick. Maria was perhaps eighteen or nineteen. She must have been here three or four years at least. 'So – you know the family well?'

'*Si, señorita*.'

Susannah caught her lower lip between her teeth. 'And – do you like working for Señor and Señora d'Alvarez?'

'*Si, señorita*.'

Clearly, Maria had no intention of gossiping and Susannah gave up the struggle. She would know soon enough. It was just that name – Don Fernando. And Cuevas! But surely there were many Don Fernandos in Spain.

She finished her coffee, Maria collected the tray and then led the way down the winding staircase to the corridor below. Now Susannah's eyes were drawn to the floodlit fountains in the courtyard, and the scores of flying insects dancing about the brilliance.

They crossed the hall Susannah had seen earlier and entered the corridor at the opposite side, halting after only a few moments at a panelled white door. Maria tapped lightly on the panels with her nails, and a voice called: *'Entrar!'*

Susannah hung back. It didn't sound like Monica d'Alvarez at all, but Maria was urging her forward.

'Señorita King, *señora*,' she announced politely, and Susannah found herself propelled inside and the door closed firmly behind her.

The woman seated on a low striped couch was most definitely not Monica d'Alvarez. She was much older for one thing, easily seventy, and totally Latin in appearance, with elegantly styled hair and a pale, aristocratic face. Around her lined throat, her wrists, her fingers was a veritable fortune in diamonds, and she rose to her feet with unconscious dignity.

'Ah, Señorita King,' she observed, in cold modulated tones. 'Please to come and sit down. I trust you had a comfortable journey.'

Susannah stepped forward reluctantly, looking helplessly about her. The room was huge by normal standards, with tapestry-hung walls and more of the Moorish arches evident in the window frames. The carpet underfoot was of a fine Chinese design, and in the lacquered cabinets that lined the walls she could see collections of china and jade. An enormous fireplace with a marble sill drew attention to the portrait of a young woman above, while the empty grate itself was concealed behind a magnificent Japanese screen. She had the ridiculous idea that she had come to the wrong house, that this woman could not be Señora d'Alvarez, that some terrible mistake had been made.

But the woman was taking her hand and shaking it, albeit fleetingly, indicating that she should sit in the armchair opposite. Then she reseated herself and subjected Susannah to an intent scrutiny.

'So?' she said at last. 'You are to teach Marla.'

Susannah swallowed with difficulty. 'Yes, *señora*.'

'You realize, do you not, that we do not approve?'

Susannah's bewilderment grew. 'We?' she echoed faintly.

'Of course, *señorita*. My nephew and myself.' She frowned as Susannah continued to look blank. 'The child's father, *señorita*!'

'Oh! Oh, I see.' At last something was beginning to make sense.

'My nephew's wife – she is impulsive, *señorita*.' The old woman forced a smile, but Susannah sensed the hostility behind it. 'She does not appreciate that Marla's position as my nephew's heir necessitates that she should be brought up to take her place at the head of the company. It is unfortunate that there is no male heir to the estate, but . . .' She gave a shrug that was purely continental in origin.

Susannah licked her dry lips. 'Perhaps – perhaps the fact that – Señora d'Alvarez is an American—'

'Marla is not an American, *señorita*!' The old woman was very definite about that.

'No, *señora*.'

'You may be wondering why I am telling you this, *señorita*,' she continued. 'It is because I wish you to know at the outset that so far as Marla's father and myself are concerned this arrangement you have made with – with Señora d'Alvarez cannot be of a lasting duration, do you understand?'

Susannah caught her breath. 'You're – dismissing me, *señora*?'

The old woman's lips curled. 'Don Fernando will ask you to leave, *señorita*, not I. I am merely warning you that you would be unwise to expect to stay here longer than a few days.'

Susannah rose to her feet, suddenly stifled by the scarcely veiled antagonism. 'If that is all, *señora*—'

'That is all, *señorita*.'

The *señora* was completely in control of herself, whereas Susannah felt hot and upset, not to say embarrassed. Surely if this was the situation here, Monica d'Alvarez should have had more sense than to engage a governess without first consulting either her husband or his aunt. And where was Monica anyway? Why couldn't she have been here to meet her instead of this aristocratic old – old harridan?

'You may go, *señorita*,' the *señora* was saying now.

'My nephew will no doubt wish to interview you himself before you meet Marla. Perhaps later would be suitable – after dinner, *si*? We will let you know.'

Susannah didn't answer. There was nothing to say. Señora d'Alvarez – if indeed that was her name – had a way of making statements that brooked no argument.

She went to the door reaching for the handle, but before she touched it it turned, and she stepped back quickly to avoid being struck as the door swung inwards.

It was suddenly as though all the blood was draining out of her face, and afterwards she wondered however she had managed not to make some startled ejaculation. But a man had entered the room – a tall, lean, dark man – a man whose image was indelibly printed on her memory. Dressed all in black – black silk shirt, open at the throat, black breeches that clung to him like a second skin, and thrust into black-knee-length boots. There was no mistaking his identity.

As Susannah stood there as though carved from stone, he ignored her, looking past her to the old woman who had risen to face them. It was then that she realized that he was not shocked at finding her here – that he had known of her arrival – that it was he who had stood in the shadows while Pedro was taking her suitcases out of the car . . .

CHAPTER EIGHT

SUSANNAH wondered how she could ever have thought her bedroom attractive. She hated it, she hated everything about it; she hated this beautiful house; but most of all she hated Fernando d'Alvarez!

She paced restlessly about the room, unable to sit down, unable to even think coherently, and certainly unable to eat any of the delicious dinner which Maria had brought up on a tray half an hour ago. She was empty, certainly, but it was an emptiness more of the spirit than of the body.

What a fool she had been, she told herself over and over again. She ought to have known – she ought to have guessed that there were too many coincidences for them all to be accidental. Fernando was Monica's husband, incredibly; and Marla's father ...

Her breath caught on a sob. She thought she would never forget the way that Fernando had looked at her when his aunt introduced them a little over an hour ago. There had been cold anger and contempt in his eyes – in *his* eyes, when it should have have been she who was feeling angry and contemptuous – of *him*!

She sank down into a chair and buried her face in her hands. Thank God that his aunt didn't want her here, that he himself didn't want an English governess for the child. How could she have stayed here – seeing him every day, watching him with Monica, teaching *their* child!

She couldn't remain seated. She had to think – to *think*! And oh, God! where was Monica? And when would she be coming back?

A knock came at the balcony door and she started violently. But it was only Maria, and Susannah opened the door wide, indicating that she could take away the untouched tray.

But Maria shook her head at the tray. "No, *señorita*.

Don Fernando wishes to see you now. Please to come with me.'

Susannah stared at her disbelievingly. 'Don Fernando – wishes to see me?' she echoed.

'*Si, señorita*. If you have finished your dinner, *naturalmente*.'

Susannah pressed a hand to her churning stomach. 'I – I wasn't hungry,' she murmured awkwardly.

Maria shrugged. 'Then we will go, *si*?'

'I suppose so.'

What choice did she have? Susannah asked herself. Since leaving the room downstairs where Señora d'Alvarez had interviewed her, she had been expecting some sort of a dismissal, not a summons.

They went downstairs to the lower corridor and Maria indicated another door some distance along. '*El estidio de Don Fernando, señorita*,' she said, pointing, and Susannah understood enough to know that this was Fernando's study. This time it was left to her to knock and await his command, and when it came it was with much reluctance that she entered the book-lined room.

Fernando was standing by the windows, his back to her, his dark head outlined against the ruby red velvet of the curtains. He did not even trouble to turn and look at her as she closed the door, but said harshly: '*Sit down, señorita!*' an uncompromising order.

Susannah remained standing, hovering near the door, ready for escape if need be, and heard the swift intake of breath from someone else in the room. She looked round and saw a girl seated in an armchair in the far corner of the room, her presence not immediately discernible in the shadowy lamplight. Pale, sallow features, straight black hair confined in a single braid over one shoulder, a somewhat old-fashioned dress of wine-coloured silk – it had to be Marla, and Susannah wondered whether she had been brought here deliberately to witness the dismissal.

Fernando turned then and surveyed her with unconcealed impatience. 'Please,' he said, 'sit – down, señorita.'

Please!

She remembered him saying that word before – pleading with her to look at him, to see him again, to forgive him, to go to Wendcombe with him . . .

Deciding that her legs were not at all reliable just at this moment, Susannah sought a straight-backed chair with arms carved like claws. Then she faced him, summoning all her pride and composure. All right, he was married, that accounted for all the peculiar reactions he had made to her innocent comments, but she was not to blame for his disloyalty. She had been unaware that all the time he was making love to her he was not free to do so. No wonder he had said he did not want to hurt her, did not want to defile her innocence! He had known he had no right to arouse her untried emotions. But was that the only reason for the grim contempt she had glimpsed earlier, or was it simply that he was angry that she had found him out in his deception?

'Now . . .' Fernando came to his desk which stood squarely in the centre of the floor, a dominant piece of furniture in mahogany and leather. 'I understand my aunt has told you that my – wife engaged you without our foreknowledge, *señorita*.'

Susannah stiffened. So that was how it was to be – as it had been before in that other room with the old Señora d'Alvarez. They were to behave as strangers. She curled her nails into her palms remembering something else – one small item of information about himself which he had volunteered. When his mother had died, his father's sister had come to take charge of the family – the woman who had interviewed Susannah had to be that sister, the aunt of whom Fernando had spoken so emotionlessly. Having met her, Susannah could understand how intimidating she must have seemed to a boy of ten! And yet now it seemed he and his aunt were allied against his wife . . .

'*Señorita?*'

Susannah realized with a sense of shock that Fernando was waiting for her reply and that she had been sitting staring into space, scarcely aware of her surroundings in those few moments.

'I – yes. Yes, she had.'

Fernando's eyes narrowed. 'Marla is a pupil at the Convent de l'Asuncion. I cannot imagine why my wife should imagine she requires further tuition.'

Susannah straightened her back. 'You wife thought it might be preferable for Marla to learn a little more about the world from a different viewpoint, *señor*.'

'Indeed?' Fernando's eyes moved past her to rest for a moment on the girl curled in the armchair in the corner.

Susannah glanced round at Marla also. In England a girl of Marla's age would have had something to say for herself on this subject. But Marla sat, impassive, waiting for someone else to make the decisions. Susannah began to think that perhaps Monica d'Alvarez had a point after all. And she should have been here to raise it. But as she apparently was not . . .

She turned to Fernando again. 'I think your wife considers the Spanish way of education somewhat – restrictive, *señor*.'

Fernando's fist came down on the desk hard, and his eyes flashed dangerously as he held her gaze. 'I am perfectly aware of my wife's opinions of all things Spanish!' he snapped savagely.

'Yes, *señor*.' Susannah's voice was barely audible, and she had to force herself not to shrink from the fury in his face.

'So,' Fernando rested his palms on the leather surface of his desk, gaining control of himself again. 'So, *señorita*; and what is your opinion?'

Susannah drew an unsteady breath. She would have no opinions in this matter. Her main objective was to leave this house as quickly as possible. But when she took a moment to glance at Marla again she had to be honest.

'I – I agree with your wife, *señor*,' she replied quietly.

'You do?'

'Yes.' She took another breath. 'And in any case, shouldn't Marla have – have the right to say something for herself? Er – *señor*!'

Fernando straightened, a scowl marring his lean features. 'Marla is happy at the convent, *señorita*.'

'Is she?' Susannah couldn't prevent the words or the dryness of her tone.

'Why do you doubt it?' he demanded, his eyes dark and intense.

'Why do you not?' Susannah clenched her fists. 'Have you asked her?'

Fernando took a cheroot out of the carved ivory box on his desk and put it between his teeth, lighting it with a silver lighter. His expression was brooding and Susannah wondered why she didn't just get up and walk out of here. By talking with him, arguing with him – albeit about Marla's future – she was involving herself in his affairs and they were not and could not be anything to do with her. It was a pity that Monica d'Alvarez was not present. Then she could have seen how futile was her determination to change Marla's future.

Fernando drew deeply on his cheroot and then beckoned the girl to him. Marla slid obediently from her chair and came to stand beside him, tall for her age and slim, her features bearing a very slight resemblance to his own.

'*Ahora*, Marla,' he said encouragingly, 'you have heard what Señorita King has said, have you not? She believes that you may not be happy at the convent.' He frowned. 'Are you?'

'*Si*, Papa.'

Fernando raised dark eyebrows. 'Is that the truth, Marla?'

'*Si*, Papa.'

Fernando inclined his head towards Susannah and she felt a rising sense of frustration. She had changed her mind, too. Asking Marla whether she was happy at the convent was not going to solving anything, not when the child was brought up to obey her elders implicitly. She might well be happy there, or perhaps untroubled was a more honest description. But how could she decide when she was offered no alternative?

Pushing back her chair, Susannah rose to her feet. 'If

that is all, señor, I'll go back to my room and pack my belongings. I will have to throw myself on your hospitality for tonight, but I'll telephone for transport in the morning and leave as early as I can—'

'*Basta!*' Fernando's voice was harsh and angry, and for an instant Susannah saw something violent in the depths of his eyes. 'Do not be in such a hurry, *señorita*. You cannot leave here until my wife returns. She employed you, not I.'

'But Señora d'Alvarez said—'

'I care not what Señora d'Alvarez said, *señorita*. You will remain here, at least until my wife returns.'

Susannah found it hard to breathe. 'And when will that be?'

'I do not know for sure, *señorita*. A few days, a week – who knows when Monica will choose to return to the boredom of my house!'

Susannah turned a startled gaze on Marla, but there was no emotion in her face. If she had heard and understood what her father had just said, it meant nothing to her. Susannah's throat was parched. 'I – I cannot stay here, *señor*—'

'I am afraid you must, *señorita*.' There was an implacable hardness about him now.

Susannah looked again at Marla. 'How do you propose to enforce that, *señor*?' she asked tautly.

Fernando's lips twisted. 'Do you owe no sense of loyalty to my wife, *señorita*? I understand that she paid you a month's salary in advance to ensure that you did not change your mind.'

Susannah's cheeks flamed. She had forgotten Monica's generosity, her eagerness to have her teach her daughter.

'I – I will repay it,' she began awkwardly, but he shook his head.

'I think not. You will stay, *señorita*. If you are as – concerned for Marla as you pretend, then you should regard this as a challenge!'

Susannah twisted her hands together. 'You know I can't stay—'

His eyes were cold. 'I know nothing of the kind, *señorita*. Are you or are you not the kind of young woman who – how do you say it – gives up at the first obstacle?'

Susannah caught her breath. He was deliberately goading her, challenging her; they might have been the strangers he was pretending them to be.

'I – I –' She looked at Marla despairingly. 'Does – does your daughter want me to stay?'

Fernando looked down at Marla. 'Well?' he asked. 'Would you like Señorita King to stay? Shall I arrange for you to have leave of absence from the convent so that you can take lessons with the *señorita*?'

Marla's lips parted, but her eyelids veiled her expression. 'If that is what you want, Papa,' she said dutifully.

Susannah shook her head, and half turned away. 'Very well, *señor*. You leave me no choice.'

Fernando pressed out the stub of his cheroot in an onyx ashtray. 'You came here to do a job, *señorita*. Just because the – er – conditions are not as you expected it does not mean that the task should be abandoned.'

Susannah swung round to face him, anger overcoming her despair. 'You aunt gave me to understand that I was not wanted here, *señor*. I see nothing in your attitude to change that opinion.'

'Nevertheless, it is decided. You will stay until Monica's return.'

'And what are my duties to be?' Susannah spread a helpless hand. '*Señor*, I cannot teach Marla in the way the convent has been teaching her. Were I staying it would be different. We would have a routine – work out a schedule. How can you expect me to achieve anything in such a limited period of time?'

'That can be decided, *señorita*,' he answered shortly. 'I suggest we leave the details until tomorrow morning. Marla is tired, and so, I am sure, are you.'

Susannah was tired, she was exhausted, but she doubted whether several hours spent sleepless in that comfortable bed upstairs would make a scrap of difference to her condition.

'May I go, then, *señor*?' she inquired, unable to withstand any more of this barbed verbal fencing.

Fernando hesitated, and then he shrugged. 'If you wish, *señorita*.'

'Thank you.' Susannah walked jerkily towards the door, conscious of his eyes following her. As she opened the door she looked back. 'Good night, *señor*. Good night, Marla.'

The girl looked up, and a faint smile touched her pale lips. 'Good night, *señorita*,' she said politely.

Susannah did not sleep well, but at least she did sleep even though her dreams were punctuated with bouts of restlessness that brought her awake, hot and sweating, staring into the darkness with desperate eyes.

She had expected Fernando to get rid of her at the first opportunity, but he was forcing her to stay! It didn't make sense. His attitude when he had first encountered her had shown his contempt for her presence, so why was he now inventing obstacles to prevent her departure? It was obvious that he did not really want her here – he *could not* want her here – and she for her part had no wish to stay. She had been foolishly naïve imagining a man like Fernando Cuevas might not be married in a country where family life meant such a lot. But he had seemed so sincere and she had wanted to believe that he was unattached. And yet now, everything remembered pointed to the existence of his wife. He had said so little about himself for one thing, never discussed his home or his family except from the distance of years when he had spoken about his own childhood. He had never suggested that she might write to him, or visit him in Spain, and she went cold when she considered how nearly she had come to making a complete fool of herself. And the night they had spent together at the cottage in Wendcombe, his wife had been only a couple of hours' drive away at the Castana house.

She rolled on to her stomach and buried her face in the pillows. At least he had not taken advantage of her inno-

115

cence; his conscience must have asserted itself at the last moment. And it hardly seemed possible after the way he had treated her this evening that once he had been eager to hold her in his arms, to kiss her intimately, to make her overwhelmingly aware of his physical need of her.

Even thinking such thoughts caused a wave of heat to envelop her body and she moved her legs restively. She wondered what he would have done if she had attempted to renew that kind of relationship with him here. Or had he been afraid that that was what she intended, and had invited Marla to join him to avoid such difficulties?

Thinking of Marla brought Susannah's thoughts to Monica d'Alvarez once more. Where was she? She had known the date Susannah was due to arrive. They had corresponded. So why had she chosen this particular time to be absent? Unless she was with Max Rosenberg . . .

Susannah turned on to her back again. What had Lucia said about Monica and Max Rosenberg? Until now she had not been interested, but suddenly she needed to remember. And why? she asked herself bitterly. To justify Fernando's behaviour – with her.

She heaved a sigh. Nevertheless, Monica had seen a lot of the man while she was staying with the Castanas, nothing could alter that. He was, Susannah supposed, in his middle fifties, and Lucie had disparagingly dismissed him as one of Monica's starving artists. She had not elaborated upon his talents except to say that Spain had a surfeit of such hangers-on, and Susannah had not been sufficiently bothered to find out. All the same, if Monica was as old as Susannah had thought her to be, she was considerably older than her husband, and maybe she found consolation in the belief that other men still found her attractive.

But to say that was to presuppose that Fernando no longer found her attractive, and Susannah did not know that. On the contrary, the fact that he had written that letter repudiating any association with her pointed to his wanting to sustain his marriage. And certainly this evening he had behaved as any husband would have behaved confronted by a situation contrived by his wife. Except

116

. . . She frowned into the darkness. Except when she had asked about Monica's return. Then a little of his bitterness had shown. But whether that bitterness was directed towards himself or his wife, she could not know.

She must have fallen into a deep sleep just before dawn, because she didn't wake until brilliant sunlight swept across her bed as Maria threw back the curtains and opened the shutters.

'*Buenos dias, señorita,*' she greeted Susannah cheerfully. 'It is after eight o'clock, and Señora Gomez said you would wish to be up, *si*?'

Susannah propped herself up on her elbows, blinking and raising a hand to shade her eyes. 'Thank you, I would.' She reached for her watch from the bedside table and saw a tray on which reposed a pot of coffee, hot rolls under a perspex cover, curls of butter and conserve. 'Oh – is this for me?'

Maria nodded and smiled. '*Si, señorita.*'

Susannah dragged herself into a sitting position and examined the face of the watch she had retrieved. Twenty past eight! It couldn't be! But it was.

'Tell me,' she said, sliding her legs from beneath the covers to sit on the side of the bed next to the tray, 'what time does Señorita Marla usually leave for the convent?'

Maria paused by the door. 'The *señorita* begins lessons at eight o'clock, after mass, *señorita.*'

'Eight o'clock!' Susannah shook her head confusedly. 'And has – has she gone to the convent today?'

'No, *señorita.* Don Fernando say you are to teach Señorita Marla for a little, *si*?'

'I suppose so.' Susannah didn't sound enthusiastic.

Maria went out of the door, but stopped again as Susannah called: 'What do I do – I mean, after breakfast? Where am I to teach the *señorita*?'

'There is a room, *señorita*, for the *niña*. Perhaps you will use that.'

'And can you show me where it is, Maria?'

Maria hesitated. 'I think I will speak with Señora Gomez, *señorita.* She will know what you must do. I will

117

come back and tell you what she says, *si?*'

'Please,' Susannah smiled. 'You're very kind.'

'*De nada.*'

Maria wanted no thanks and after she had gone Susannah poured herself some of the delicious-smelling coffee and buttered a roll. She had not eaten since lunch-time the previous day and in spite of everything that had happened her naturally healthy body required sus-tenance. Somehow, with the sun streaming through her windows, warming even the tiles of the floor, and the scents of the hanging blossoms on the balcony pervading the atmosphere with their redolent perfumes, it was not possible to remain completely dispirited.

After two rolls and three cups of coffee she felt infinitely more ready to face the day. She showered and dressed in the grey skirt and white blouse she had worn as uniform in England. She brushed her hair, coiling it into a knot at the nape of her neck with several pins. She used make-up sparingly and was ready and waiting when Maria returned. If the Spanish girl thought the trans-formation from tumbled sleepiness to businesslike neat-ness rather startling she concealed it admirably and said:

'I am to take you to Señorita Marla, *señorita*. Will you come with me.'

To Susannah's surprise, Maria led her back to the room where the elderly Señora d'Alvarez had interviewed her the evening before. She couldn't help the way her nerves tightened as Maria first knocked at and then opened the door, but she need not have been alarmed. There was no sign of the old matriarch this morning. Marla was alone.

The door closed behind the maid and Susannah stood for a moment just looking at her charge. Marla was seated neatly on the edge of an armchair, her hands folded in her lap. She was wearing a navy blue dress with a heavily pleated skirt and a pristine white collar. It was a very warm morning, and Susannah in her thin blouse and skirt was feeling the heat, while Marla, in her long-sleeved dress, appeared totally unconcerned. And yet for all that, Susannah was appalled that a child of her age should not expose more of her limbs to the sun.

'Good morning, Marla,' she said, at last, as the girl continued to look down at her hands folded in her lap.

Marla lifted her chin. '*Buenos dias, señorita,*' she replied politely.

Susannah took a deep breath. 'Well, I suggest we get to know one another, don't you?'

'*Si, señorita.*'

'And I think we should begin by speaking English, Marla.'

'Yes, Miss King.'

Susannah glanced round. They were getting nowhere fast.

'Is this where we are to do our lessons, Marla?'

'No, Miss King.'

'Then where are we to work? Has your – father left any instructions for me?'

Marla linked her fingers together. 'We are to work in the studio upstairs, Miss King. But this morning, my father thought you might like to see more of the *casa* – the house.'

'I see,' Susannah nodded, relieved. 'I'm sorry if I've kept you waiting.'

Marla shrugged. 'My father made no stipulation as to time, Miss King.'

'No. No, I know he didn't, but . . .' Susannah broke off. This would not do. A governess was always in command. She sighed. 'Well – where shall we begin?'

Marla rose to her feet. 'Would you like to see the pool?'

'The pool?' Susannah raised dark eyebrows. 'I didn't know there was a pool.'

Marla allowed a slight smile to curve her lips. 'Come with me,' she directed. 'I will show you.'

They went outside, into the brilliant sunlight which even at this hour of the morning possessed a fierceness never felt in cooler climes. Now Susannah could see that the balcony which shadowed the courtyard was supported by a series of pillars forming arches between. Beneath the balcony was a cloistered walk, and she was glad to seek its coolness. Stone seats edged the fountains, and as the sunlight reflected in the water it sparkled iridescently, dropping in tiny globules on the leaves of bougainvillea that spilled its blossoms round the rim. Hanging baskets of fuchsia and geranium provided vivid splashes of colour adding a European touch to purely Moorish architecture.

Marla followed the shade of the balcony to where another arched way, similar to the one Susannah and Pedro had used to gain access the night before, gave on to yet another courtyard. The building was much bigger than Susannah had realized. It was not simply the rectangular shape with its fourth side missing as she had imagined, but instead an E-shaped structure with two inner courtyards.

A magnificent pool almost filled the central area, reflecting the tracery of the inevitable arches that flanked it. Tiling in an intricate design of blue and green and gold surrounded the edge of the pool, but although it looked inviting, Susannah guessed that no one ever used it for bathing.

The pool was overlooked by another balcony, and noticing the numerous shuttered windows here, Susannah decided that the greater part of the house was never used. It seemed a pity that so much beauty should be appreciated by so few people. And yet, perhaps, not everyone would consider such architectural austerity beautiful. But Susannah loved the simple lines, the predominance of geometric design, its regular symmetry. The pool was shielded by a row of cypress trees which formed a fourth side to the square.

Marla was watching her companion's reactions closely. 'You find it appealing?' she asked.

Susannah nodded. 'It's beautiful.'

'Yes, beautiful,' agreed Marla, with satisfaction, showing more enthusiasm than Susannah would have thought possible.

Susannah's fingers curved round one of the fluted pillars that supported the gallery. 'Was it ever used? For bathing, I mean.'

Marla shook her head. 'I presume you mean in its original form.'

'Hmm.' Susannah's nails encountered the hardness of marble.

Marla frowned. 'No. I imagine it was for ornamental purposes only. The Moors never immersed themselves in water. They had water poured over them. Besides, there were bathing quarters.' She gesticulated across the courtyard. 'They even had steam rooms, like the Romans.' She smiled. 'A Moor always followed a strict routine when it came to cleansing himself. First his mouth, then his hands, then his feet.'

Susannah was intrigued. 'Go on. Why?'

Marla warmed to her subject. 'It was intended to cleanse the soul before the body. You see, the mouth speaks evil, the hands can perform evil, and the feet can take a sinner where evil is.'

Susannah smiled. 'How fascinating! Do you know a lot about the history of your country?'

Marla shrugged. 'When one lives in a Moorish palace, one tends to become obsessed with one's surroundings.'

'This is a Moorish palace!'

'It was – many years ago. Now it is simply La Casa d'Alvarez.'

She began to walk along the tiled rim of the pool and after a moment's hesitation Susannah followed her. They walked between the cypress trees and came upon formal gardens, smooth turf and borders of cream and red roses, and some trumpet-shaped flowers she could not identify. There were more of the fine cypresses, and low walls and trellises overhung with flowering vines. There was also a small pavilion which Marla explained had been built by her grandfather. Susannah wondered whether he had had it erected for Pilar, Fernando's mother, whose name was engraved on the disc that Fernando wore about his neck.

But thinking of Fernando unsettled her, and she was glad when they reached the high wall which provided an adequate barrier between the Casa d'Alvarez and the outside world and Marla suggested that they returned to the house for morning chocolate.

The rather sweet chocolate drink was not particularly to Susannah's taste, and was served in the same room they had occupied earlier. But now, much to her dismay, Susannah found the elderly Señora d'Alvarez already in residence. She looked up as they came in, and the hostility in her gaze as she looked at the older girl was very much in evidence.

Marla, unaware of any undercurrents, greeted her great-aunt politely with a chaste kiss on her wrinkled cheek, and then the old *señora* turned her sharp eyes on Susannah.

'So, *señorita*,' she said, 'you have persuaded my nephew to permit you to stay on.'

Susannah subsided into her seat. 'I – your nephew insisted I stayed until Señora d'Alvarez – Señora Monica d'Alvarez returned.'

'And why should he insist upon such a thing? He was not informed of your imminent arrival until three days ago. Why should he wish to keep you here until his wife returns?'

'Perhaps you should ask Don Fernando that, *señora*,' replied Susannah quietly, and had the satisfaction of seeing the old woman's lips purse impatiently.

'I have been showing Miss King the grounds, Tia Amalia,' put in Marla, unknowingly relieving the tension between them.

Her aunt turned to her. 'Have you? And what arrangements has your father made regarding your education while Señorita King is staying here?'

Susannah refused to rise to the bait, but Marla looked surprised. 'Miss King is to give me lessons, Tia Amalia. You know that.'

'And when are these lessons to begin? If you have spent the morning walking in the grounds you have not been attending to your studies, have you, Marla?'

Marla flushed at this and Susannah felt annoyed. The tenuous relationship she was building with the girl would not be enhanced by Señora d'Alvarez' barbed comments.

'I think it is always easier to get to know the person one is going to teach before actual instruction begins, *señora*,' she said. 'Why, even in school a class uses the first period with a new mistress discovering the other's attitudes and capabilities. Marla and I could not sit down to lessons together without learning a little about one another.'

Amalia d'Alvarez bestowed her with a contemptuous stare. 'And what have you learned about my niece, *señorita*?'

Susannah sighed. 'I'd rather not discuss my impressions, *señora*.'

'Ah, I see. It is impressions we are discussing.'

Susannah curbed the desire to tell the *señora* exactly what she thought of *her* at least, and Marla, who was looking somewhat discomfited, set about pouring her aunt's chocolate from a tall china jug.

As they drank the excessively sweet beverage Susannah looked around the room. The jade figurines in the lacquered cabinet attracted her attention but she was loath to make any comment about them that Señora d'Alvarez might deliberately misconstrue. So she contented herself with following the oriental design of the carpet until the fire-screen caught her eye.

The scene depicted, and painstakingly worked, on its tapestry surface was that of two women and a man in the gardens of a pagoda-like dwelling. Below the curling eaves of the building there were tiny bridges over narrow streams, and arbors sheltered by cherry trees, their blossom so real, Susannah thought, that you could almost smell it. The figures in the foreground were real, too. Only their costume was outdated.

Marla finished her chocolate and puting down her cup said: 'Do you like Japanese art, too, Miss King?'

Susannah turned to look at her. 'I like beautiful things, Marla. And there are many beautiful things here.'

Marla rose to her feet and walked over to the fireplace. 'My father brought this screen back from Osaka many years ago. I believe it is very valuable. It is quite old, too. Perhaps three-hundred years.'

Susannah was impressed. 'The colours are so rich!'

Marla went on, 'Of course it was restored here in Spain.'

'Oh, I see,' Susannah nodded.

'Do you like it?'

'Very much.'

'But do you know what it depicts? See – this is the Silver Pavilion, and can you see this figure hiding behind her parasol? The man is her lover. But it is a futile relationship. You see, he is married – to this woman here – the one who teases him with her fan, so?'

Susannah felt a painful stirring of her emotions. In a few short sentences Marla had unknowingly described the association between Fernando, Monica and herself. The Japanese screen depicted faithfully the cruel twist of fate which had put her into the position of the other woman . . .

CHAPTER NINE

SUSANNAH ate a solitary lunch in her room.

After taking morning chocolate with them, Amalia d'Alvarez had asked Marla to assist her to her apartments, and when after half an hour Marla had not come back, Susannah had made her own way along the corridor and up the winding staircase to her own sanctuary.

When Maria came to take away her tray, she informed Susannah that the Señorita Marla always rested for a while after lunch, and that she should do likewise.

'Dona Amalia takes tea on the patio at four o'clock, *señorita*, and Señorita Marla joins her there.'

Susannah made a helpless gesture. 'Am I expected to do so?'

'I do not know, *señorita*. I would think not.'

Susannah gave an involuntary ejaculation. 'Then when am I expected to spend time with Marla?' she exclaimed.

Maria looked scandalized at Susannah's casual use of her charge's given name, but she replied: 'Señorita Marla does not take lessons in the afternoon, *señorita*.'

Susannah was impatient. 'And what am I expected to do for the rest of the day?' she demanded. She could hardly be expected to stay in her room all the time. But on the other hand, would they permit her to go walking alone – outside the confining walls of the *casa*? If Monica d'Alvarez had been here she could have asked her. But then, if Monica d'Alvarez was here, she would not . . .

Maria was looking most upset, and with a sense of contrition Susannah realized she ought not to be questioning the maid. It was nothing to do with her.

'Never mind,' she said now, shaking her head. 'I'll work something out. Thank you, Maria.'

'*Si, señorita*.' Maria hesitated by the door. 'Perhaps you should discuss this with Don Fernando, *señorita*.'

Susannah sighed. 'Perhaps I should at that.' Her nerves

tautened at the mere thought of talking with him again. 'Where is he? In his study?'

Maria shook her head vigorously. 'Oh, no, *señorita*, Don Fernando is away today, at the vineyards – or perhaps at his office in Cadiz.'

Susannah flung herself into a chair. 'I see. Very well, I – I'll speak to him later.'

'*Si, señorita.*'

After Maria had gone, Susannah got up again and paced about the room. It was very hot, and on impulse she took off the confining skirt and blouse and went to take another shower. Then she dressed in a simple shift of yellow cotton and fastening her hair with two elastic bands she went down the stairs to the lower corridor.

In this *siesta* hour the house was very quiet, and even her sandalled feet seemed to echo on the tiles. She found a door that opened into the courtyard and keeping in the shade of the balcony walked towards the arched way which led into the other courtyard.

With the sun almost completely overhead, the pool gleamed coolly, and she wished it was a swimming pool that she might immerse herself in its depths. But as she walked to the brink and looked down into the water she saw that it was barely two feet deep, and that although the water sparkled it was far from lucid.

Sighing, she walked along the side and through the cypress trees into the gardens. Taking the path which led to the small pavilion, she halted before its fragile structure closely hedged about with climbing plants and shrubs. Then on impulse, she climbed the steps and entered its shadowy interior.

Long creepers wound about the tall pillars which supported its domed roof, and there were stone seats and a central fountain which no longer shed its spray into the round stone basin. There was something rather melancholy about the neglected walls and crumbling stonework and when a lizard, disturbed by Susannah's entrance, ran swiftly across the floor within inches of her bare toes she gasped and quickly emerged into the sunshine.

She made her way back to her room eventually, and sat on her bed wondering whether she ought to make some attempt to speak to Fernando later. Surely he must know that she would feel lost and aimless without any set routine to adhere to, or didn't he care? After all, it had not been his idea that she should come here, and Monica had made it sound much different from the reality. Or perhaps she hadn't. Perhaps it was simply that Susannah had wanted to come in the hope of meeting Fernando again, and everything connected with Spain had seemed that much larger than life.

In fact, it was two days before Susannah saw Fernando again, two days during which the pattern of her life so long as she remained at the Casa d'Alvarez was made apparent to her.

In the mornings, she and Marla were expected to do lessons together in the large studio at the top of the stairs which Marla explained was used by her mother when she was at home. It was a light airy apartment, plain walls adorned only with colour prints which Monica herself had designed. There were canvases and easels, but Susannah and Marla sat at the wide table and worked from the comprehensive array of text books Monica had provided.

Lunch was taken late, in the Spanish fashion, and afterwards she was expected to entertain herself and not intrude in any way upon the usual routine of the household.

It was a most unsatisfactory arrangement, thought Susannah, not least because Marla herself was left almost entirely in the company of Señora Amalia d'Alvarez during the late afternoon after her *siesta* and in the evening before she went to bed. It was not healthy that a girl of Marla's age should spend so much time with an elderly woman, and it was not surprising that she became quiet and subdued. Susannah was beginning to suspect that from Marla's point of view the convent provided a better balance. At least that way she spent a part of the day with girls of her own age.

But when Susannah accepted this post she had been unaware of the confined circumstances the girl lived under, and as each day passed she became more and more resentful on Marla's behalf. The child was only half alive. What she needed wasn't a governess, but a companion, someone with whom she could romp and play and behave as any normal fourteen-year-old ought to behave. Her childhood was slipping by, unnoticed, while she sat quietly with an old woman, sharing her reminiscences of the past.

Susannah would have liked to have discussed the matter with Fernando, but he was never around. Maria, her only contact apart from Marla herself, explained that Don Fernando left the *casa* quite early in the morning and recently had taken to returning late in the evenings. Susannah couldn't help but wonder whether this was to avoid any chance of their meeting one another, but she was appalled to consider that the only time Marla saw her father was at dinner, and never without the company of Amalia d'Alvarez.

On Saturday of that week, Marla told Susannah that on Sunday morning there would be no lessons. She was to attend mass at the church in the village with Tia Amalia and her father, and therefore Susannah was free for the day.

Free! Susannah could have laughed. How could she be free when as yet she had not even put a foot outside the walls of the Casa d'Alvarez!

But she was glad for Marla's sake that this was to be an outing with her father. She had gauged from the girl's attitude throughout the last couple of days that Marla thought a great deal of her father, much more, apparently, than of her mother. Not wanting to probe, Susannah had not asked her about her association with Monica, but it was impossible not to notice that she did not figure very frequently in Marla's conversation.

Susannah washed her hair on Sunday morning. She sat on her balcony while the rest of the family was out and dried it in the hot sunshine. Already she was acquiring a light tan and she thought longingly of a beach somewhere and the cooling surge of the surf.

After lunch, she dragged her chair back into the bedroom and settled down with a book. But she was restless, and she knew it was because she was conscious of Fernando's presence. During the past few days his constant absence had served as a kind of salve to her spirit, but now, knowing he was about somewhere, made it impossible for her to relax. Sooner or later she would have to speak to him – alone, and he must know that as well as she did.

Towards half past three she brushed her hair, secured it with the hairpins on her nape, and examined her appearance in the mirror. She was not wearing her usual skirt and blouse today, but the cream cotton tunic was reasonably smart and it was impossible to wear tights in this heat. She looked as businesslike as dark-fringed eyes, silver-blonde hair and a wide attractive mouth would allow, and in any case Fernando was not likely to pay a great deal of attention to her appearance when he heard what she had to say.

She went quietly down the stairs to the lower corridor and stopped before the door to Fernando's study. Raising her hand she hesitated a moment and then knocked, rather loudly. There was no immediate response and her heart sank. Of course, he probably adhered to the *siesta* habit, too. She turned away, and as she did so she heard footsteps coming along the corridor. She glanced round, her heart thumping, and encountered the gaze of the man who had been occupying her thoughts.

Fernando was looking curiously alien this afternoon in a black suit, the jacket of which reached only to his waist. He wore a while silk shirt and there were ruffles of lace at his throat. His boots were knee-length and highly polished, and she wondered whether he intended going riding.

'*Buenas tardes, señorita,*' he greeted her, without expression. 'You wished to see me?'

'Yes – yes, *señor.*'

Fernando's lips curled. 'I regret I do not have time to speak with you now, *señorita.* I am just on my way out.

My aunt and Marla are waiting in the car.'

'You're going out?' Susannah felt a ridiculous pang of desolation. 'But—' She paused. 'I never seem able to get in touch with you.'

Fernando frowned. 'I did not think we had anything to say to one another, *señorita*. I understand from Marla that your lessons are going well—'

Susannah turned away. 'Yes. Yes, they are,' she said shortly. 'We spend at least *three hours* every day in each other's company. I – I find it all most hectic!'

The bitterness in her tones got through to him. 'You are bored, *señorita*?'

Susannah faced him. 'And if I am?'

'I regret, we do not have a great deal to offer in the way of entertainment, *señorita*.'

'Oh, you don't understand,' she exclaimed, making a futile gesture. 'Look, I want to talk to you. What have I to do? Make an appointment?'

Fernando scowled. 'Do not be impertinent, *señorita*. I am available every evening.'

'Are you?' Susannah was fast losing the desire to remain calm. She was angry with him and she wanted to show it. 'I thought you were avoiding me!'

Fernando glanced over his shoulder as though afraid someone might come upon them unexpectedly. 'I must go,' he insisted briefly. 'But you may come to my study at nine-thirty this evening, if that is suitable to you.'

'Thank you.'

Fernando hesitated. 'We are going to the bullfight. You would not enjoy the spectacle.'

'Are you asking me or telling me?' she inquired, defiance in her eyes.

Fernando's fists clenched. 'Until this evening, *señorita*,' he stated formally, and walked away down the corridor without looking back.

Susannah turned towards the stairs, but as she did so she realized that Marla was accompanying Fernando and his aunt to the bullfight. She felt slightly sick. If it was not a spectacle for her, how could he consider taking a child to see it?

By the time she reached her room, however, these thoughts had been superseded by other anxieties. She had had no right to speak to Fernando as she had. He had not invited her to come to the Casa d'Alvarez, and their situations here were vastly different from in England even without the added complication of his marriage. Besides, she should have known better, she who had always prided herself on not getting involved.

Dinner was served in her room at eight-thirty, and by nine-thirty she was a mass of nerves. She had known this would happen, of course. That was why she had gone to see Fernando earlier on the spur of the moment before she had had a chance to have second thoughts. Now she had them in plenty, and a worrying sense of inadequacy.

She had changed out of the dress she had worn earlier into a long straight amber-patterned gown which was completely plain apart from the two slits at the sides. It fastened round her slim waist with a sash and drew attention to the curving line of her hips. She tied back her hair with a chiffon scarf, checked her make-up, and then descended the stairs to the lower corridor.

Fernando answered her tentative knock immediately, opening the study door himself, and standing back so that she could enter the room. He closed the door behind her and Susannah stood in the centre of the room feeling rather like a schoolgirl summoned to the headmaster's study for some misdemeanour. But at least he was alone, of that she had assured herself in those first few seconds.

Fernando walked behind his desk as though deliberately placing a barrier between them, effectively signifying that this was no personal assignation. He gestured towards a chair opposite him. 'Won't you sit down, *señorita*?'

Susannah hesitated, and then went forward to sit where he had suggested, folding her hands in her lap. Fernando leant forward to extract a cheroot from the box on the desk and her eyes were drawn to the brown skin rising from the opened neck of his dark blue silk shirt. He, too, had changed from his previous attire and now a wine red velvet jacket clothed his broad shoulders. He had a sombre arrogance and she marvelled at her own temerity in coming here. How could she have imagined that things remained the same? That people didn't change? But even so, she could never have been expected to appreciate the whole circumstances of this affair.

Fernando lit the cheroot to his satisfaction and then seated himself in the black leather swivel chair at his side of the desk. 'Now, *señorita*,' he began, with all the cool assurance of his breeding, 'why did you wish to see me?'

Susannah looked down at her hands. So the charade was to go on. If she let it . . .

She looked up. 'I wanted to speak to you about Marla, *señor*.'

'Yes?'

He was superbly confident, and she wondered if the decanter of brandy at his elbow had anything to do with it.

'Yes,' she said now, forcing herself to speak as coolly as he did. 'Our — that is, the arrangement for Marla's tuition is not very satisfactory, *señor*.'

'No?' He frowned through a veil of tobacco smoke. 'Why not? I understand it works very well.'

'And from whom do you understand that?' she asked shortly, forgetting for a moment to say *señor*.

Fernando's dark brows drew more closely together. 'My aunt keeps me informed of your progress, *señorita*.'

'Yes, I thought she might.' Susannah's nails dug into her palms. 'However, I disagree.'

'With what? Her reports on your progress?'

Susannah swallowed the ready retort that sprang to her lips. 'No,' she denied carefully, 'I disagree that the arrangement works well, *señor*.'

Fernando's nostrils flared. 'I see.' He paused. 'And of course you can elaborate on that.'

'Of course.'

'Then go ahead.'

'Marla spends too much time in the company of – of Señora d'Alvarez – your aunt.'

'What has that to do with the unsatisfactory arrangements for her tuition, *señorita*?'

Susannah sighed. 'You're deliberately misunderstanding me, *señor*.'

'Am I?'

'You know you are!'

Susannah felt frustrated. She was trembling and she took several deep breaths, trying to calm herself. This would never do. She would get nowhere if she didn't argue coolly and sensibly, and not allow him to disconcert her.

Pressing her moist palms down upon her knees, she went on quietly: 'Marla and I are only permitted to see each other in the mornings, *señor*. At twelve o'clock we are expected to join your aunt for chocolate, and after that . . .' she spread her hands. 'I'm expendable.'

Fernando rested his elbow on the desk and regarded her closely. 'And are you not perhaps confusing your own boredom with the quality of Marla's education—'

'No!' Susannah clenched her fists. 'No, I'm not. There's more to being a governess than sitting in a schoolroom giving lessons. Marla and I should have some free time together. We could go to the coast. Swim! Play tennis! Mix with other people!'

The heavy lids with their thick lashes veiled his gaze. 'Marla is no different from any other girl of her age and background.'

'In Spain, I suppose you mean.'

'*Naturalmente, señorita.*'

Susannah sighed. 'Well, I think it's unnatural! The clothes she wears! The hours she spends just sitting and listening to Señora d'Alvarez talking about the past! It's unhealthy!'

'*Señorita*, you forget yourself!'

He was angry now, but Susannah didn't care. How could anyone be so blind? Marla was being stifled in this atmosphere. She was already half-way to becoming a facsimile of her great-aunt.

'Don't you think, remembering your own childhood, that Marla should be allowed a little more freedom?' she exclaimed urgently. 'You said yourself—'

'*Basta!*' Fernando's fist came down hard on the desk and he rose to his feet. 'We are not concerned with me, *señorita*, only with Marla. What would you have me say? That she should run free with you like some charity child?'

Susannah uttered a strangled gasp at the callousness of his words, and suddenly he seemed to realize exactly what he had said.

'*Por dios*, Susannah,' he muttered, 'I did not mean that!'

Susannah rose to her feet and grasping the back of her chair dragged herself behind it, supporting herself as she faced him.

'I don't think there is anything more to be said, *señor*,' she managed chokingly. 'It's obvious the opinion you have of me. Very well, I'll make no more pleas on Marla's behalf. I can even appreciate why she makes no attempt to plead with you herself.'

'*Susannah!*' A pulse was throbbing noticeably near his jawline. 'Susannah, you do not understand—'

'No, I don't. I don't understand how you can say the things you do, feel the way you do, and yet still persist in keeping me here until your wife returns? What is it? Some sort of perverted justice?'

She stared at him bitterly for a long time and finally his eyes fell before hers. He stubbed his cheroot out savagely in the onyx ashtray, and said: 'You should not have come here, Susannah.'

She gestured impotently. 'Do you think I don't know that?'

'Then why did you?' He looked at her again, his eyes mirroring a little of the anguish of mind he was experiencing.

She moved her shoulders helplessly. 'I've asked myself that several times.'

Fernando flexed his shoulder muscles wearily. '*Dios*, you must have known we were bound to meet! What good has it done? Could you not have accepted that when I left England, what had been between us was over – irrevocably.'

Susannah's fingers probed the fine veneer of wood on the back of the chair. 'Do you imagine I would have come here if I had known you were Monica's husband?' she exclaimed painfully. 'How could I connect Fernando Cuevas with Don Fernando d'Alvarez?'

'Did it matter whose husband I was? I was married. Was that not enough?' he demanded.

Susannah's lips parted in dismay. 'Do you think I knew that?'

Perplexity clouded his eyes. 'What do you mean?'

'Dear heaven, Fernando, I didn't know you were married! Do you imagine I would have agreed to – to our spending a weekend together if I had thought—' She broke off, pressing a hand to her throat. 'Oh, God! What kind of a woman do you think I am?'

She stumbled towards the door, but his voice halted her.

'Am I expected to believe that you didn't know?'

She turned, holding her head erect. 'I don't actually care what you believe, *señor*,' she stated tremulously. 'And as I already know *how* you think of me, *what* you think of me doesn't seem very important!'

'*Susannah!*' His harsh tones could still generate a devastating current of awareness along her veins. 'You worked for the Castanas. Do you really mean to tell me that Lucie never regaled you with my history?'

'Why should she?' Susannah's knees felt disturbingly unsteady. 'You were never a subject for discussion between Señora Castana and myself. I am sorry to disappoint you—'

'Be silent!' He came round the desk, his hands clenching and unclenching at his sides. 'Surely you must have known . . .'

'Why? How? How could I? You didn't say anything. You seldom spoke about yourself at all. And I thought you were merely reticent. How wrong you can be!'

Fernando moved his head disbelievingly from side to

135

side. 'But my letter – the letter I left behind—'

'What of it?' Susannah's voice almost broke then. 'I cherished that letter. I foolishly imagined that because you thought you were too old for me . . .' She broke off, gathering her composure. 'Well, anyway, I obviously read more into it than was intended.' She reached for the door handle. 'Can I go now?'

Fernando took another step towards her, but then a kind of iron self-control hardened his mouth and he halted abruptly. He stood for a moment just looking at her, and then, drawing a deep breath, he said: 'I find your explanation – difficult to believe, and yet . . .' He shook his head. 'I must reconsider. The situation calls for it.' He tugged absently at the hair at the nape of his neck. 'You wished to leave, did you not? I will make the necessary arrangements at once.'

Susannah couldn't believe her ears. 'You're dismissing me?'

'Is that not what you wanted?'

'Yes – no – that is—' Susannah put a bewildered hand to her head. 'I – I can't go now. At least, I'll stay a little longer. For Marla's sake.'

His scowl returned. 'Why? You said yourself that the arrangements were not to your liking.'

'No. But they could be. Don't you see?' She moved her arms desperately. 'Fernando, I'm not a puppet to be manipulated at will. I came here to do a job, and I should like the chance to do it. Give me a chance! Besides, what will Marla think if I suddenly depart?'

'Marla will accept what I tell her.'

'Oh, yes, of course she will. I'd forgotten the more ridiculous aspects of the situation. Marla will do exactly as you tell her, won't she? Poor misguided creature!'

'Have a care, Susannah!'

His jaw was taut, and she felt an unexpected quiver of anticipation run through her. Suddenly their situations were reversed and she had only just realized it.

Linking her fingers together, she said: 'If you love your daughter, you must know she's not happy.'

He gestured impatiently. 'How can you say that? Has

she said so?'

Susannah moved her shoulders. 'No. She's too – subdued to say a thing like that. And that in itself should be proof enough. Dear heaven, why do you spend so little time with her? Leaving her constantly to the care of an unsympathetic old woman—'

'You overreach yourself, *señorita*,' he snapped coldly. 'None of this concerns you!'

'I disagree.' Susannah held up her head. 'When I came here – before you forced me into a position of becoming involved with Marla – your affairs meant nothing to me. Now they do. Now I've got to know Marla, to like her, to realize that she's being stifled in this cloying atmosphere—'

'That is enough!'

'No, it's not.' Susannah was becoming more and more reckless. 'You made me stay here. You created this situation. Now you'll have to face the consequences. What are you afraid of? That Marla will let the Alvarez family down? Or that she'll exhibit a little of the spirit you always used to have—'

Fernando crossed the space between them in two strides, his face twisted with rage. 'Do not dare to stand there and say such things to me!' he ground out furiously. 'What right have you to stand in judgment on things of which you know nothing?'

He glared down at her, and for a moment she thought he was about to strike her. But then he turned away, breathing heavily.

'This conversation is getting us nowhere, *señorita*,' he said, through clenched teeth. 'You will please to go to your room and pack your belongings. I will have Morales drive you to Seville in the morning. It should not be too difficult for you to get a flight back to England. I will see that you are generously reimbursed for your trouble!'

'*No!*' Susannah stared at him desperately. 'Fernando, I won't go back to England. All right, I accept that *our* relationship is over, but at least let me try to help your daughter. Give me a chance to show you how happy Marla could be.'

'It is impossible!' His tone was harsh.

'Why? Why is it?' Susannah felt like shaking him. 'If – if Marla's mother was here she would agree with me!'

Fernando turned to face her. 'Oh, yes, I am sure,' he nodded bitterly. 'But perhaps you should ask her why she spends so little time with the girl. If she is so concerned for Marla's welfare, why does she disappear for weeks on end without word?'

Susannah bent her head. 'That's nothing to do with me.'

'I agree. None of this is anything to do with you. So go!'

'And what will you tell your wife when she eventually does come back? That you found my services unsatisfactory? Or that as I had known you in London, I was becoming an embarrassment to you?'

Fernando's face grew even grimmer. 'What are you saying now? That if I do not accede to your demands you will tell my wife of our association?'

Susannah gasped. That he should think such a thing of *her*! She stared at him for several agonized seconds and then she realized that he did not really think that at all. He was simply saying it to put her on the defensive, to achieve what plain speaking had not been able to achieve. But there were possibilities which even she had not considered until now.

Taking a deep breath, she said: 'Would you call that bargaining power, Fernando?'

His fists clenched. 'You would *use* it!'

Susannah shrugged. 'Give me two weeks with Marla. Two weeks of freedom. Not from lessons – they'd continue as usual. But allow us some time to get away from the *casa*.'

'And if – Monica returns in the meantime?'

Susannah bent her head. It would not be easy. Her impulsiveness had not considered the possibility of Monica's return. For some reason she had expected her to be away.

But Fernando was awaiting her answer, and she could not let him see how deeply she was disturbed by him even now.

'You can say you're employing me for a – probationary period,' she ventured at last.

He made a disgusted sound. 'You realize I can report this conversation to the *policia*, do you not? I believe it is known as – blackmail!'

Susannah winced. 'Do not be so dramatic, Fernando. What am I asking, after all? Two weeks – out of a life-time of years!'

There was silence for a few minutes and then he turned and walked back to his desk. She saw with a sense of contrition that there was a curiously defeated air about him, and she longed to go to him and comfort him and show him how much she loved him still.

But she could not. She no longer believed the things he had told her in London. It had been expedient to tell her he loved her, but it had almost ruined her life, and she was being incredibly foolish even staying here and risking further humiliation. But Marla was his daughter, and Susannah's compassion for her outweighed her own anxieties.

'Very well, *señorita*,' he said heavily, taking another cheroot from the box. 'You may stay.'

'And the arrangements?'

'I will permit Morales to drive you where you want to go, *señorita*. But you are not to leave the car except in his company, and if you disobey these instructions Morales will report to me.'

Susannah sighed. She had won. But what a hollow victory!

CHAPTER TEN

THE following morning, Marla was astonished when Susannah told her that after her *siesta* that afternoon they were going out.

'But where are we going, Miss King?' she asked in surprise. 'Tia Amalia expects me to take tea with her on the patio at four o'clock.'

Susannah forced a smile. 'I know. But your father has given us permission to go for a drive with Morales. Doesn't the idea appeal to you?'

Marla was clearly fighting with her loyalties. 'Of course, I should enjoy going for a drive, Miss King, but Tia Amalia may not wish to do so.'

'Tia Amalia!' Susannah caught back the retort that came to her lips. 'Marla, there is just to be – the two of us. Not Tia Amalia as well.'

Marla looked, if anything, even more astounded. 'We are to go out alone, Miss King?'

'Well, if you can call going with Morales alone, I suppose so.'

Marla shook her head. 'But what will Tia Amalia say? Does she know?'

'I doubt it.' Susannah's tone was dry. Then she tried to instil a little enthusiasm into the girl. 'Marla, we could go to Cadiz. I've never been there. I'm longing to see something of the countryside around the *casa*. You can show me!'

Marla still looked hesitant. 'And my father permits this?'

Susannah controlled her impatience. 'Why not?'

Marla shrugged. 'Always I go out with Tia Amalia.'

'Before I came, I agree. But, Marla, I'm just as capable of taking you out as – as Tia Amalia.'

Marla looked at her doubtfully. 'If Papa is agreeable . . .' she murmured.

'He is.' Susannah lifted her shoulders. 'Marla, try and

think of this expedition as – as an adventure. Something exciting and enjoyable – and not to be taken too seriously.'

A smile touched Marla's pale lips. 'I will try, Miss King. But I do not think Tia Amalia will be very pleased.'

Amalia d'Alvarez was not pleased, indeed, she was positively furious. 'What can Fernando be thinking of?' she demanded coldly, her narrowed eyes moving from her great-niece to the unwelcome figure of Susannah seated on the couch, quietly drinking her morning chocolate. 'Besides, Marla always keeps me company in the afternoons, do you not, Marla? Do my needs matter so little when compared to an outing with Señorita King?'

Marla looked terribly uncomfortable. 'It was Papa's idea, Tia Amalia,' she stressed urgently, and Susannah did not contradict her. 'And tomorrow I will take tea with you as usual.'

Susannah bit her lips to prevent herself from disabusing her of that idea. Sufficient unto the day, she thought wryly. And if Marla enjoyed herself this afternoon perhaps it would be easier tomorrow. Perhaps even Señora d'Alvarez would concede a point if Marla was enthusiastic, but that was carrying wishful thinking a little too far, she realized. It was evident from the old woman's expression that she knew at whose door to lay the blame for this change of circumstances, and Susannah had no doubt that she would do everything in her power to make Fernando withdraw his approval.

All the same, nothing could completely douse the feeling of excited anticipation she felt that afternoon as she and Marla climbed into the back of the sleek cream open tourer Pedro Morales had brought to the entrance to meet them. Susannah had determinedly shed her more formal clothes for a short red pleated skirt and a white ribbed cotton sweater, and Marla, in her dark green dress of silk jersey, looked rather sombre beside her.

But if Marla was conscious of their differences in appearance she made no comment upon it, and gave Susannah her usual controlled smile as Pedro sounded his horn and the tall gates in the high wall were opened for them.

The heat of the day was subsiding a little, and the movement of the car created a slight breeze which lifted the weight of Susannah's hair and tore it out of its confining knot. She had to content herself with looping it behind her ears, but even this was useless as they drove along and she gave up and allowed it its freedom. Marla's hair was, as usual, confined in the single braid, and Susannah longed to see it loose about her shoulders. With the right clothes, and a less restrictive attitude, Marla would be very attractive, and it seemed a terrible shame that no one, not even Monica, had seen this and done something about it. As it was the girl looked plain and dowdy, and much too old for her ten years.

Cadiz lay on a peninsula, separated from the mainland town of San Fernando by a narrow isthmus. For some distance before reaching the peninsula they had been following the coastline, and the sea looked incredibly blue and inviting beneath the cloudless sky. They passed villages along the way, that had changed little for centuries, where gardens rioted with colour and donkeys still provided a necessary means of transport. The scents of the flowers were intoxicating and not until the salty tang of brine invaded their nostrils did they shed their perfume.

Cadiz itself was definitely African in appearance, a fitting reminder of its violent history. There was a predominance of white-painted buildings, some with cupolas that glinted in the sunlight. There were churches standing in oases of green, and palm trees that spread their smooth leaves towards the enormous landlocked harbour that sprawled along the city's inner boundaries. There were parks where one could sit and look out over the Gulf of Cadiz and colourful markets where traders plied their produce – from the silvery sardines brought into the harbour to delicate necklaces of gold and silver filigree made across the straits in North Africa. It was a busy, brawling port contrasting its narrow, over-crowded streets with quiet squares.

Pedro drove through the city, pointing out the ruined watch towers set at intervals as a protection in olden days, and even Marla became enthusiastic as she caught sight of the vessels in the harbour. Susannah saw a stall with oranges and wanted Pedro to stop, but he drove on to park on the Alameda, a promenade overlooking the sea.

Susannah leant forward and touched his shoulder. 'Can we get out?' she asked.

Pedro looked doubtful. '*Por que, señorita?*'

Susannah sighed. 'To walk for a while. Surely you don't expect to take us straight back to the *casa*, do you?'

Pedro frowned, looking confused. Clearly he had not understood everything she had said, and Marla, after a moment's hesitation, translated for him. Pedro listened, and then made an involuntary movement of his hands, saying something in a rapid patois that Susannah could only guess at.

Marla shook her head. 'Pedro says it would be better if we permitted him to drive us wherever we want to go, *señorita.*'

Susannah felt impatient. 'But the exercise would do us good.' She looked all round. 'There are people walking here. What harm does he expect can come to us?'

Marla half smiled. 'Would you like to see the *catedral* instead? We could walk there.'

Susannah looked at her. 'You mean inside, of course,' and at Marla's nod she acquiesced. 'Why not? I would like to see the cathedral.'

They spent almost an hour going over the building which had been constructed during the seventeenth and eighteenth centuries; a Christian temple in purely Moslem surroundings. In spite of her earlier annoyance Susannah could not remain unmoved by the red and white marble pillars that supported the roof, or the domed vault which carried the weight of the High Altar. Marla who had, she said, been to the cathedral many times with her father, told Susannah a little of its history and explained that the huge monstrance which had been made in the seventeenth century, and which was easily the most valuable article among the treasures of the cathedral, was carried in procession through the city every year on the feast of Corpus Christi.

It was almost seven o'clock when they arrived back at the Casa d'Alvarez, but Marla seemed unconcerned. Throughout the hours they had been away, she had become more and more talkative, exhibiting an intelligence which was both sharp and instructive. She was showing how much she had absorbed and had never found any outlet for until now. Susannah allowed her to speak unrestrainedly, only occasionally putting in some opinion of her own. She was realizing that Marla's problem lay in this lack of communication with either her aunt or her father, and the confidence she was now displaying must be allowed to develop. She couldn't help but feel delighted at the success of the outing. She only wished she could go to Fernando and show him this other side to his daughter.

The following morning Señora d'Alvarez was unusually silent when Marla tentatively explained that she and Miss King were going out again that afternoon. Susannah guessed that she had spoken to Fernando and that he had explained the alteration in the present arrangements. The old woman contented herself with casting malevolent glances in Susannah's direction, and the girl had no doubt that she would be blamed entirely for this unwelcome state of affairs.

But Susannah did not spend too long worrying over Amalia d'Alvarez. The outings were a success, and Marla grew more enthusiastic daily. They went to Algeciras and Jerez, they saw the vineyards whose grapes produced the wine for which this area was famous, and on one special occasion they left immediately after breakfast and drove to Seville to see the cathedral and the Alcazar. If Marla saw it all simply as a way of showing her governess a little of the beauty of this part of the world, Susannah did not mind. The less obvious the attempt to arouse Marla from her apathy, to turn her from a shy introvert into a spirited teenager, the better.

Susannah had even coaxed her to her room and one

afternoon she encouraged the Spanish girl to try on some of her clothes. Although Marla was much younger, she was quite tall and well built for her age, and as Susannah was very slim her clothes fitted quite well – sufficiently so to enable Marla to see how attractive she could be in casual slacks and sweaters.

'Papa would never permit me to wear anything like this,' she said regretfully. 'Besides, Tia Amalia would never agree.'

Susannah studied her thoughtfully. 'If I shortened those trousers,' she murmured, half to herself, 'you could have them. I seldom wear them. Green isn't my favourite colour. And I've got loads of ribbed sweaters like the one you're wearing. You can have that, too, if you like.'

Marla gasped, 'You're not serious!'

'Why not? Don't you like them?'

'You know I do.' Marla looked at her reflection with troubled eyes. 'But what shall I say to Papa?'

'Tell him to mind his own business!' remarked a cool voice from the doorway, and both girls swung round in amazement.

'Mama!' gasped Marla in horror.

'Señora d'Alvarez!' Susannah was astounded. 'When did you get back?'

Monica d'Alvarez shrugged and strolled lazily into the room. 'Half an hour ago, I guess,' she replied, looking round at the strewn garments. 'You've been having some fashion parade! What goes on?'

Marla hesitated, looking at Susannah, and Susannah saw the confidence draining out of her. Rushing into speech, she said:

'Marla has just been trying on a few of my things. I've been showing her how much less – confining – casual clothes can be.'

Monica glanced down at her own shirt and slacks and nodded. 'I've been trying to tell her that for years,' she observed dryly.

'Yes, well—' Susannah felt awkward. 'Perhaps Marla needed to see herself to be convinced.'

'Maybe so.' Monica took out her cigarettes and lit one.

'In any case, I'm pleased to see you're making some progress, Miss King. I'm sorry I wasn't here when you arrived, but . . .' She made a dismissing gesture. 'Perhaps it was just as well. I can see you've settled into the job very well.'

Susannah wished Marla would say something, but the younger girl was standing stiffly, clearly embarrassed, and totally incapable of relaxing with her mother. Susannah, who until then had thought that perhaps Marla had more in common with her mother, now saw how wrong she had been. They were totally different. Monica, with her brashness, her lack of sensitivity, would never understand the complex individual who was her daughter, and Marla could only be hurt by her mother's lack of perception. Although Susannah shared Monica's concern for her daughter's subjugation in this household, Marla would never turn out to be the kind of girl Monica wanted her to be. And for that Susannah found she was thankful.

Now she said: 'Marla and I have been spending a lot of time together, haven't we, Marla?' The girl nodded, and Susannah went on: 'I suppose you have spoken to – to your husband since your return.'

'Yeah!' Monica flicked ash carelessly on to the tiled floor. 'I've spoken to him. I guess it was pretty rough on you to begin with. I thought it might be.'

And that's why you went away, thought Susannah dryly, beginning to understand Monica a little better.

Monica flicked her gaze to her daughter. 'You surely do look more like my daughter in those clothes,' she commented mockingly.

'What is going on here!'

Fernando was standing in the open doorway, dark and alien in the black garb he seemed to prefer, a riding crop hanging from his long fingers.

Marla could not have looked more distressed and Susannah wanted to rave at both her parents to get out of here and leave the girl alone. But of course she could not, and in any case it was Monica who spoke first.

'Marla's been trying on a few of Miss King's clothes, honey,' she drawled with evident satisfaction. 'Don't you

146

think she looks cute?'

'*Señorita!*' Fernando ignored his wife. 'What is the meaning of this?'

Susannah heaved a sigh. 'The meaning of what, *señor*? As your – as your wife has just said, Marla was just seeing how she looked in slacks and a sweater.'

Fernando looked at the other garments draped about the room. 'And these things, *señorita*? Do you normally leave your belongings strewn about like this?'

Susannah avoided his glittering eyes. 'No. No, of course not.'

'So am I to understand that Marla has been trying all these garments?'

'Some of them.'

Fernando struck his boot angrily with his crop. 'And what explanation can you give for such – such irresponsible behaviour?'

'Oh, really, Fernando,' exclaimed Monica, in a bored tone. 'Must we make an inquisition out of it? Where's the harm? All girls like dressing up!'

'I agree,' Susannah nodded. She looked at Marla. 'We were just having fun, weren't we?'

Marla was silent for so long that Susannah thought she was too shocked to say anything, but then, amazingly, she said: 'That's right, Papa. We were having – fun.' She took a step forward. 'Do you not think that these clothes are attractive, Papa? My dresses are all so – so old-fashioned. Miss King said so.'

'Good for Miss King!' commented Monica delightedly, but Fernando scowled.

'Miss King is not here to instruct you in the manner of dress, Marla,' he stated coldly. 'Nor, might I add, do I approve of you putting on someone else's clothes, whether for fun or otherwise.' He flicked an angry look in Susannah's direction. 'In future, *señorita*, you will restrict your educative powers to the schoolroom!'

Monica gave an impatient snort. 'For God's sake, Fernando, let them be! Why shouldn't Marla choose what she wants to wear? She has very little choice in anything else, heaven knows!'

Fernando turned to his wife. 'Please leave this to me, Monica. I will not have Marla upset unnecessarily.'

'You're the one who's upsetting her,' retorted Monica shortly.

Fernando's face was grim. 'Marla was perfectly happy until you began interfering with things that do not concern you, Monica. Just because, from time to time, you feel the need to behave a little more as her mother should behave, do not presume to think that this gives you any rights on her behalf! Confine your activities to the things you do best!'

'Why, you – you *swine*!' Monica's lips were clenched. She seemed unconscious of Susannah's presence. 'One of these days – one of these days—'

'You will leave? I know.' Fernando's mouth curved contemptuously. 'However, until that day comes, you will leave Marla's affairs to me!'

As Monica replied angrily to his denunciation, Susannah wished the floor would simply open up and swallow her. This was terrible! She didn't want to stand here listening to Fernando and Monica demonstrating the irretrievable breakdown of their marriage. She didn't want to be involved. She didn't want to take sides. And yet, listening to them, it was almost impossible not to do so. It was obvious, it had been obvious since Susannah's arrival, that Marla cared little for her mother, and if Monica spent so little time with her daughter what could she expect?

But Fernando soon called a halt to their argument. He, at least, was conscious of the effect it might have on Marla herself, and with another flick of his crop against his boot, he said:

'Put on your own clothes, Marla. I am on my way to the *cortijo*. I thought you might like to come with me.'

Marla was galvanized into action. 'Oh, yes, Papa,' she exclaimed, her earlier disappointment at Fernando's reception of her appearance forgotten apparently. She quickly thrust off the offending sweater and trousers in Susannah's bathroom and emerged in the plain brown muslin she had been wearing when she came to

Susannah's room. 'I am ready, Papa.'

Fernando cast a ruminative glance at the two women and then with a slight, almost imperceptible shrug of his shoulders he indicated that Marla should precede him out of the room.

After he had gone, Susannah didn't know what to say, so she began gathering the strewn garments together, folding them into neat piles. Monica watched for a few minutes and then she said:

'Well? Aren't you going to say anything?'

Susannah fastened the zip on a pair of jeans. 'No, *señora*. It's nothing to do with me.'

'Oh, don't give me that! You know perfectly well that you've formed opinions, just like anyone else. What do you think of my charming husband here? Do you think he's changed from your conception of him in England?'

Susannah felt the hot colour burning in her cheeks. 'Wh – what?' she stammered.

'I asked whether you thought Fernando was different here than in England.'

Susannah hugged the sweater she had been folding to her. 'How – how do you know I – knew your husband in England?' she faltered.

Monica stubbed out her cigarette in a nearby ashtray and lit another. 'How do you think?' she exclaimed irritably. 'Lucie told me.'

'Lu – *oh*!' Susannah felt weak at the knees. 'Señora Castana!' she murmured with relief.

Monica looked up from her cigarette, her eyes narrowed. 'Sure, Lucie told me. She'd have told me anything to prevent me from employing you.'

Susannah turned away so that Monica should not see how her hands were trembling. 'What did – Señora Castana say?' she asked, hoping she was displaying a mild interest.

Monica sniffed. 'Oh, just that Fernando had taken you and their boy out one day. To the zoo, wasn't it?'

'Yes, that's right.' Susannah pushed sweaters into a drawer.

'Yeah! Well, anyway, what did you think of him?'

'Who?'

'Fernando, of course.'

'Oh!' Susannah made a helpless movement of her shoulders. 'I– I thought he was – very nice.'

Monica wrinkled her nose. 'Nice? That's hardly a word I'd have used to describe my husband, but never mind. You realize, I suppose, that part of Lucie's maliciousness is due to the fact that she always had a hankering for him herself?'

Susannah forced a faint smile. 'Did she?'

'Yes.' Monica looked down at the glowing tip of her cigarette. 'He might have married her, too, if I hadn't happened along.'

Susannah wished she would go. She had no desire to hear Monica reminiscing about her early association with Fernando. In fact, she didn't want to talk about Fernando at all. She glanced surreptitiously at her watch, but Monica saw her and rose from where she had been lounging on the edge of the dressing table.

'Okay,' she said amiably, her ill temper banished with Fernando's departure, 'I'm going. I guess I can't expect you to understand the complexities of our relationship. If you knew the whole story, you'd probably be shocked out of your tiny mind.' She grinned. 'Oh, don't look so worried. Between us, we'll have Marla behaving like any other kid before long, you'll see.'

Susannah closed the door behind her and leaned back against it wearily. What an exhausting period it had been! She felt completely enervated, and she sank down weakly on to her bed with a depressing feeling of defeat.

No matter what Monica might say, Susannah was beginning to doubt that it was possible to achieve any lasting success in a couple of weeks with Marla. But of course, Monica was probably still unaware of the limited terms of Susannah's employment. She thought she was staying indefinitely, it appeared, and had no doubt decided that the installation of the English governess had been achieved with the minimum amount of effort. And if that were so, why hadn't Fernando disabused her? Monica had said she had seen him before seeking out the two girls. Was their relationship such that they were never civil to one another?

Susannah lay back, raising her arm to shade her eyes. And what did she think, now that Monica had returned? Their association was far worse than Fernando's occasional bouts of bitterness had led her to believe, and she wondered what part Max Rosenberg had played in the deterioration of their relationship. How long had Monica known him? How long had she behaved with this complete lack of respect for either her husband or her family?

Susannah's mind probed the endless possibilities while her sensibilities revolted against remaining in such a household. If their marriage was so abhorrent to both of them, why didn't they end it? Surely that would be the kindest thing to do for Marla's sake. But she could answer her own question. Fernando, at least, was a Roman Catholic. His church did not recognize divorce. So far as he was concerned, the vows he had made were totally binding.

A pain like a knife twisted in her stomach at this realization. For him there was no escape. She wondered whether things between herself and Fernando would have been different if he had not cared about his religion. Or was she deluding herself about his feelings for her? Certainly since she came here he had regarded her with less than contempt.

She shook her head. There was so much she didn't understand, could only guess at. Never, in any circumstances, would she have imagined Monica to be the kind of woman to attract Fernando. She was so coarse, so hard, so completely different from him. She was attractive, it was true, but she was also at least ten years older than he was, and must have been in her thirties when they married.

Susannah dragged herself up off the bed and began putting the rest of her clothes away. There was no point in trying to find answers to questions that should not even

151

concern her. Perhaps she ought to consider leaving immediately. Now that Monica was home there was bound to be more problems, and she no longer felt as though she had the strength to face them.

The following morning, Monica came to the studio while Susannah was giving Marla her morning lessons.

'You didn't join us for dinner yesterday evening,' she remarked, addressing herself to Susannah in her usual pointed way.

Susannah looked up from an English grammar and frowned. 'I beg your pardon, *señora*?'

Monica grimaced. 'I said – you didn't join us for dinner yesterday evening, Miss King.'

Susannah put down her pen. 'No, *señora*.'

'Why? Because I'm home? Or because you've had enough of eating dinner with my husband and his old dragon of an aunt?'

Susannah glanced meaningfully at Marla, but Monica seemed unperturbed, lighting one of the long American cigarettes she favoured.

'I take all my meals in my room, *señora*,' said Susannah at last.

'In your room?' Monica's head jerked up. 'You mean all these past days you've been eating in your room?'

'Yes, *señora*.'

'My God!' Monica raised her eyes heavenward. 'My husband's dictate, I suppose.'

'I don't know, *señora*. The housekeeper said—'

'Oh, Señora Gomez.' Monica nodded. 'She receives her instructions from Doña Amalia, of course.'

'It really doesn't matter, *señora*—'

'I disagree.' Monica tapped her foot impatiently. 'It matters to me. A governess is very often treated as a member of the family. If the children are young – well, then the governess sometimes takes her meals with them in the nursery. But when the child is of Marla's age and takes her meals with her parents then the governess should do the same.'

'I really don't think—'

Monica silenced her with an imperative stare. 'In future,

Miss King, you will take your meals with the family, do you understand?'

'Is that an order, *señora*?' asked Susannah, with a sigh.

'It is my wish, Miss King.'

Susannah bent her head. 'Very well.'

'Good.'

After Monica had gone, it was extremely difficult for Susannah to resume her concentration, and Marla looked at her sympathetically.

'Mama wishes to oppose Papa in all things, Miss King,' she said, showing an amazing amount of perception. 'So it is with the schooling. If Papa had wanted a governess for me, Mama would have found the convent infinitely more appealing.'

Susannah frowned. 'And you accept this, Marla?'

The girl sighed, doodling absently on the pad in front of her. 'Most of the time there is only Papa,' she replied quietly. 'Mama is away a lot.'

Susannah shook her head. 'Do you talk to your father about your mother?'

Marla looked up. 'Oh, no, Papa would never permit that. But I understand things are not easy for him.'

Susannah was astounded. For a girl of her age, Marla was startlingly adult. She had already had evidence of the intellect behind the dark eyes so disturbingly like her father's. Had she been wrong about her all along? Had she unconsciously taken Monica's biased opinion as her own? And what could Monica really know about her daughter anyway?

Susannah flicked over the pages of the English grammar. There were changes needed here, she must not lose sight of that. Marla was left too long in the company of her aunt – she was allowed little freedom. But Marla herself was not suffering as Susannah had once thought she must be suffering. On the contrary, Susannah found herself wondering ironically whether in fact Marla was not more contented in her way than the whole of the rest of them put together.

At noon they took chocolate with Amalia d'Alvarez as

usual. As soon as the maid who had brought the tray of chocolate had departed and Marla was engrossed in pouring it out, the old woman turned to Susannah and said:

'I suppose you will be leaving us soon now, *señorita*,' in satisfied tones.

Susannah forced herself to meet the cold, glittering gaze of the other woman. 'I expect I shall,' she conceded quietly.

'When? Tomorrow? The day after?'

Susannah gasped. 'Perhaps in a week, *señora*.'

'A week!' Doña Amalia snapped her finger. 'But I understood you to say that my nephew had agreed to your staying until his wife returned. As Señora d'Alvarez has returned . . .' She spread her hands.

Susannah took the cup of chocolate Marla handed to her and thanked her, playing for time. Trying to maintain a composure she was far from feeling, she said: 'Don – Don Fernando has agreed to a trial period, *señora*—'

'A trial period, *señorita!*' Doña Amalia frowned. 'I have heard nothing of this.'

Marla seated herself beside her aunt on the couch. 'Miss King is to join us for meals, too, Tia Amalia,' she said quietly.

Doña Amalia's fingers shook as she replaced her cup in its saucer. 'At whose instigation, Marla? Hers – or your mother's?'

Susannah flushed brilliantly. 'I have no wish to join your table, *señora*—' she was protesting, when Marla went on:

'Mama says that in England a governess is treated as a member of the family, Tia Amalia. Could we not do that also?'

Her aunt plucked impatiently at the several strings of pearls about her gnarled throat. 'This is not England, Marla. We do not wish to adopt English ways.'

'Mama is English, Tia Amalia.'

'You mother is American, *niña*,' retorted Doña Amalia dryly. 'And you would be as well to forget it.'

The situation was not improved at lunch time when

Monica d'Alvarez joined them in the small dining-room which opened off the main hall. It was a beautiful room, as were all the rooms in the *casa*, with walls hung with turquoise silk and an ivory white table and chairs. Long curtains of green silk hung at the windows, while the moulded ceiling was covered with an exquisite mural of the arms of the Alvarez family.

But Susannah was given little opportunity to admire the artistic abilities of its creator. She was much too aware of the antagonism that existed between Monica and the elder Señora d'Alvarez, which thickened the atmosphere around them with the tangibility of cigarette smoke. Fernando, of course, was not at home, and as Monica addressed almost all her remarks to Susannah, she was forced into a position more difficult than before. Never had the *siesta* period beckoned so appealingly, and when the meal was over she escaped to her room with heartfelt relief.

Later in the day, she and Marla went driving with Pedro. At Marla's suggestion, they took the road into the hills and Susannah saw the *cortijo* where Fernando had taken his daughter the day before.

'They are sort of farmsteads,' explained Marla, as Susannah exclaimed at the isolation of it all. 'Several families share a communal livelihood, relying on one another for almost everything.'

The particular *cortijo* that Marla had indicated was set on a terrace which seemed to have been hewn out of the rocky face of the mountain itself. There was little room for cultivation and a few goats straggled up the hillside and turned to stare as the sleek cream car drove by on the rugged road.

'Does – does your father own this land?' Susannah asked, unable to hide her curiosity.

Marla smiled. 'He did. But no longer. My father says a man should own himself.'

Susannah felt a lump in her throat. 'He's right, of course.'

'My father is usually right, Miss King,' replied Marla with touching sincerity.

Susannah hesitated a long time over choosing what to wear for dinner that evening. Some of her clothes were still in England, in a trunk at Margaret French's house, and most of the things she had brought with her were for day wear. At any other time, she would not have troubled, but this evening she particularly wanted to look her best.

She eventually chose a plain gown of black silk jersey. The neckline was high at the back and low at the front, dipping to the hollow between her breasts, and the sleeves were long and full, almost mediaeval in appearance. She brushed her hair until it shone and secured it with a black net threaded with gold on the nape of her neck.

She knew, when she was ready, that she had seldom if ever looked more attractive, and the knowledge inspired a certain amount of confidence inside her. Although, since coming to Alvaridad, she had lost some weight, and although there were shadows on her cheeks, the skin that was drawn a little tighter across her bone was lightly tanned to a honey colour, and there was something hauntingly wistful about her dark-fringed eyes.

She had not considered what she would do once she was ready and was unutterably relieved when Marla arrived at her door a few moments later. The girl surveyed her appearance admiringly and then said:

'I've come to show you the way to the *salón*, Miss King. Come with me.'

Susannah smiled. 'Thank goodness. I had no idea where to go.'

Marla smiled. 'The *casa* is not so difficult to explore. But I agree, there are many rooms that are seldom used. It is a shame. But tonight we are to dine in the main dining *salón*. You will see. It is much more impressive than the smaller one we used this afternoon.'

As Susannah could scarcely imagine anything more impressive than that silk-lined room she made no reply to this, but instead complimented Marla on her choice of dress.

Marla looked down at the long-skirted sprigged cotton she had chosen and sighed. 'My mother brought me this from England last year,' she confided. 'It is not Papa's favourite gown, but I thought that you might think it suited me.'

Susannah nodded. 'It does. You look very nice.'

'So do you.' Marla glanced sideways at her as they walked along the lower corridor. 'You always do.' She paused, and then: 'I wish my mother was more like you, Miss King. Then perhaps Papa would fall in love with her and we could all live happily together.'

Susannah stared at her young charge in horror. 'Why – why do you say such a thing?' she demanded in a strangled tone, but Marla seemed totally unconcerned.

'Because it is true,' she replied in a low voice. 'My father likes you, I know he does. And I like you, too.'

Susannah's throat felt constricted. 'I – I think you're imagining things, Marla. Your – your father wants me to leave.'

Marla shrugged. 'That is because he wants me to attend the convent. It has nothing to do with you personally.'

'How can you say that?'

Marla shook her head. 'It's true. Yesterday afternoon – when he took me to see Juan and Carlos and Anna – you were supposed to come, too.'

'I was?'

'But of course. That was why he came looking for us. But then my mother was there, and I was wearing your clothes, and Papa was angry – very angry.'

'He had no need to be.'

Marla spread her hands. 'Papa buys my clothes. He is very generous. But Tia Amalia chooses them. It is not his fault if they are old-fashioned. I hurt him very much by saying that they were.'

Susannah absorbed this in silence. It sounded reasonable. But then everything Fernando said sounded reasonable. Even his suggestion that they should spend his last week-end together ...

Marla took her to the *salon* where Fernando and his aunt were waiting. There was no sign as yet of Monica, but Fernando looked stern and unapproachable in a black

157

dinner jacket and narrow-fitting trousers. A mass of lace frothed over the satin edges of his lapels, and his hair had been combed smoothly against his head. He looked devastatingly attractive and Susannah felt her senses stirring in spite of herself as his brooding gaze moved over her with deliberate slowness.

Amalia d'Alvarez was small and elegant in black lace, but she looked with distaste at Marla's white flowered dress.

'What is this, *niña*?' she exclaimed in disgust. 'Why are you not wearing the bronze linen Sophia had laid out for you?'

Before Marla could say anything however, Fernando answered his aunt. 'Leave the child alone, Amalia,' he commanded quietly. 'The dress was bought by her mother. I think she looks most attractive.'

Even Marla could not hide her surprise at this, and it was obvious that Amalia was not used to being spoken to in such a manner. Susannah sensed her anger that Fernando should have chosen to reprove her in front of someone she regarded as a mere servant, and for a moment she expected Amalia to leave. But instead, the old woman moved away to sit on a couch and Fernando turned his attention to Susannah herself.

'May I offer you a drink, *señorita*?' he asked, showing neither rage nor pleasure at her presence. 'What would you prefer?'

Susannah avoided his gaze and looked past him to the cabinet which stood wide revealing a comprehensive array of bottles and glasses. 'Perhaps – sherry?' she ventured at last, and he inclined his head and went to pour the drink for her.

Dragging her gaze from his broad back, Susannah forced an interest in her surroundings. She had never been in this room before, and like the other apartments it was much larger than a room in any ordinary house. The walls again were silk-lined, this time in a rather delicate shade of coral, with a filigree of wrought iron providing an unusual embellishment at intervals. The furniture was a complementary blending of ancient and modern, while an exquisite Aubusson carpet spread across the central area.

Her eyes returned to Fernando and watching him pour her sherry brought back vivid memories of that other occasion at the cottage when he had looked so strangely at her because she had asked for the same drink. Was that one of the occasions when he had been convinced that she knew of his life here in Alvaridad? Had he imagined she had asked for sherry to taunt him with the wine produced by his own vineyards?

Fernando returned and handed her the glass he had filled. Susannah's eyes lifted no higher than its delicate stem which was on a level with the black cummerbund he wore around his waist.

'Thank you,' she said, taking the glass with great care so that their fingers should not touch.

Fernando stood looking down at her bent head for several seconds and then with a swift indrawing of breath he turned away. It was difficult after that for Susannah to behave as though nothing had happened. Her pulses were pounding so loudly she thought they must be audible, and a weakness had invaded her knees so that she swayed slightly. She took a hasty sip of her wine in an effort to calm herself and encountered the cold, calculating gaze of Amalia d'Alvarez.

The old woman was watching her closely, there was no mistake about that, and with an awful sense of foreboding Susannah wondered whether she had intercepted that momentary lapse on Fernando's part. Or was she imagining things? Never on any occasion since she came to the Casa d'Alvarez had Fernando given her reason to suppose that the feelings he had expressed for her in England still existed. And just because, for one fleeting moment, she had sensed a certain softening in him, brought on no doubt by his genuine affection for his daughter, she should not pretend that he was drawn to her.

Monica's appearance provided a welcome distraction. In her orange chiffon gown, generously splashed with sequins, she was as gaudily plumed as a parrot among blackbirds. She seemed totally uncaring of Amalia d'Alvarez' disdainful stare, however, and of the way the old woman drew her skirts about her as though to avoid contamination. She came confidently into the room smoking one of her long American cigarettes without which she was seldom seen, and said: 'Pour me a brandy and soda, will you, Fernando? I'm parched.'

Fernando gave a slight nod of acquiescence and Monica looked round at the three female members of the group. Her eyes alighted on Marla in her cotton dress and she smiled.

'Darling! How pretty you look!' she declared warmly. 'Isn't that the dress I bought you?'

Marla nodded. 'Yes, Mama.'

Monica went towards her daughter and walked all round her, finally tugging at the single braid Marla always wore. 'If it wasn't for this,' she remarked, 'you'd look almost American, wouldn't she, Miss King?' And her gaze flicked up to Susannah.

Susannah herself had been quite content to remain in the background. She had no desire for Monica to stage a repeat performance of her luncheon tactics when she had used Susannah to say things she could otherwise not have said.

But now she moved her shoulders in a casual gesture of indifference. 'I expect it's cooler for Marla to wear her hair in a plait,' she said cautiously.

Monica made a grimace. 'Maybe so. But hell, once in a while it would be nice to see it blowing free.' She turned away as though bored with the conversation and found her husband behind her with her brandy and soda.

She took the glass without thanks and swallowed half its contents at a gulp, wiping her mouth with the back of her hand. Fernando's expression remained impassive as he went to inquire whether his aunt required another drink and then, when she refused, he took up a position next to Marla.

Monica finished her drink and waved her glass for another. 'Isn't this nice?' she observed dryly, as Fernando moved to get her the second drink. 'Everyone's having a wonderful time!'

Fernando came back with the full glass. 'I should not advise you to drink too many of those before dinner, Monica,' he commented quietly. 'You don't want to – be ill, do you?'

The words, though spoken in a low tone, were distinctly audible in the quiet room, and Susannah thought they held a meaningful warning. But Monica merely gave her husband a scornful smile and said:

'I can hold my liquor, Fernando. I don't need anyone to watch out for me. Least of all you!' She deliberately raised the glass and drank half its contents, her eyes holding his all the while. 'You see? It's too late for you to make any effort to change things now.'

Susannah half turned away, staring blindly out across the patio. She was wishing herself anywhere but here, when Monica again chose to drag her into the conversation.

'Tell me what you used to do for entertainment in London, Miss King,' she demanded, cradling her glass between her fingers. 'I expect you had lots of boy-friends, didn't you—'

'I do not think Señorita King's affairs are anything to do with you, Monica,' snapped Fernando before Susannah could say anything.

'Oh, take no notice of my stuffy husband,' drawled Monica, dismissing his protest with a wave of her hand. 'He may not be interested, but I am. I'd like to know how the average girl-about-town survives these days.'

'I'd hardly call myself the average girl-about-town,' replied Susannah awkwardly.

'Why? Didn't you like going out?'

Susannah sighed. 'Well – yes. But I liked staying in, too.' She shook her head. 'You're really talking to the wrong person. I was a terrible bore, I'm afraid.'

Monica raised her narrow plucked eyebrows. 'I wouldn't say that,' she commented, surveying the other girl critically.

'Monica, must we persist with this ridiculous discussion?' Fernando's mouth was drawn into a thin line. 'You are embarrassing Señorita King. Can you not see that?'

Monica shrugged. 'Why? I haven't asked for any intimate details, have I?' She turned back to Susannah. 'Am I embarrassing you, honey?'

Susannah looked uncomfortably towards Marla. 'I – I suppose not.'

'There you are!' Monica cast a mocking glance at her husband. 'You see, English girls are not like your subdued Spanish women. They're not afraid of leaving their families, getting flats of their own, training for careers! They enjoy their independence. Just as I want Marla to do.'

'We will leave Marla out of this,' stated Fernando ominously, but Monica ignored him.

'You'd like the chance to go to university in England, wouldn't you, darling?' she asked her daughter, touching her shoulder affectionately. 'You don't really enjoy sitting listening to Tia Amalia's monotonous tales of when she was a girl, do you?'

'That is enough, Monica!' Fernando sounded coldly furious. 'If you refuse to behave with respect for your elders, I suggest you take dinner in your room!'

Monica's eyes widened. 'Who the hell do you think you're talking to?' she demanded shrilly. 'Just because the peasants around here treat you like God, don't expect me to worship at the shrine!'

'*No haga un escandalo*, Monica,' he ground out savagely, but she merely laughed.

'Speak English, darling. Don't you want Miss King to understand the charming things you say to me when we are alone together?'

Susannah didn't know where to look, and it was with immense relief that she saw the maid, Maria, appear in the doorway to announce that dinner was served.

The meal, a cold soup called *gazpacho, tortillas* filled with a tempting mixture of mushrooms and ham, and chicken spread on a bed of fried rice, was delicious, but Susannah could not do justice to it. She had eaten rather sparingly ever since she came to live in Fernando's house, but at least she had been alone, in the quiet of her room, and able to relax away from prying eyes. But here, conscious of the intense atmosphere, aware of the undercurrents flowing about her, she found it impossible to do more than pick at her food, and she was glad when the dessert stage was reached and she could take her time peeling a peach.

Coffee was served in the *salón*, and Susannah drank hers quickly, almost burning her mouth, and then asked to be excused. Monica raised her eyebrows again at this request, and said:

'Must you rush away, Miss King? I was hoping we might continue our conversation about London. I know it well, and I'm sure we could find a lot to talk about.'

'I – I'm really rather tired—' began Susannah, shaking her head apologetically.

'Surely not.' Monica was mocking. 'I think you're afraid, Miss King. Afraid that my husband and I may embarrass you again—'

'*Sagrada Madre*, Monica, can't you leave the girl alone?' exclaimed Fernando savagely. 'Let her go to bed if she wants to do so.'

'Really, I – I am tired,' stammered Susannah uncomfortably, but Monica wouldn't let it go.

'My husband doesn't understand that I find the conversation of himself and his aunt boring in the extreme!' she declared spitefully, 'and you're my only hope of salvation from an extremely boring evening!'

Susannah caught her lower lip between her teeth. 'Please – excuse me,' she insisted, and Monica pressed out her half-smoked cigarette with an exclamation of annoyance.

'What's the point of bringing someone fresh into this ghastly household if that someone refuses to mix with us socially?' she asked, of no one in particular. 'God! Am I not sick of this place!'

Susannah moved towards the door, but Monica saw her and directed her malice towards her now.

'Yes, go!' she sneered. 'Close your ears to our little contretemps. Refuse to face facts like everyone else in this room!'

Fernando, who had been standing before the wide

hearth, now took a step forward, his fists clenched in the pockets of his jacket.

'Susannah has said she is tired, Monica!' he stated grimly. 'Is that not enough for you?'

Monica's lips parted and Susannah saw the mocking glint that entered her eyes. 'Oh!' she taunted. 'So it's *Susannah*, is it? That's her name.' She gave Susannah a speculative look. 'And how long have you been thinking of her as Susannah, darling?'

Susannah waited to hear no more. She had had enough. Let Fernando find whatever answer suited him best. She didn't want to know about it.

She walked quickly along the corridor to the staircase that led up to her room and ran upstairs on urgent feet. Only when the door of her room had closed behind her did she begin to feel the sickness that engulfed her stomach. With a groan, she went into her bathroom, retching long after it was necessary to do so.

She felt weak when it was over and her body was moist with sweat. She struggled out of her clothes and took a cooling shower, and then pulled on a navy silk wrapper and cleaned her teeth. When she returned to the bedroom she didn't bother to draw the curtains but switched out her light and stretched on the bed.

It was very dark outside, the only illumination coming from the lamps hung around the courtyard below. She lay listening to the sounds of the insects almost without being aware of doing so. There was the interminable scraping of the cicadas in the gardens beyond the cypress trees, there was the faint droning of mosquitoes as they danced with death around the lamps below the balcony, and occasionally the soft swish of wings as a huge moth flung itself against the panes of her window. She would have to get up to close the shutters, but not yet, she hadn't the strength.

What a terrible day it had been! The worst day she could ever remember, except perhaps the day Fernando had left her to return to Spain. But at least then there had been hope – now there was none.

Why on earth had Fernando married a woman like

Monica? Had he loved her all those years ago — a love that had been killed by her unfaithfulness? It seemed the only answer. And yet it was difficult to imagine someone as fastidious as Fernando choosing a woman who shared no respect for his beliefs. Or had he been different then? He had said that week-end at the cottage that his father had despaired of him. Was that what he had meant? Had he been a reckless young man, uncaring of the principles he now lived by?

Susannah heaved a sigh. It didn't really matter why he had married Monica; they were married and that was that. The sooner she accepted the fact and left the Casa d'Alvarez the better. Marla might miss her for a few days, but she would return to lessons at the convent and Susannah would soon be forgotten.

Exhaustion took its toll on her and eventually she slept, but she came awake with a start to the shadowy darkness of her room with the distinct impression that some sound had wakened her. Blinking, she sat up, and as she did so she saw a shadow move near the fitted wardrobe at the far side of the room. A cry was stifled in the throat as the figure realized he had been seen and stepped into a shaft of moonlight.

'Fernando!' she breathed in amazement. 'What are you doing here?'

CHAPTER ELEVEN

FERNANDO moved towards the bed. He had shed the dinner jacket he had been wearing earlier that evening, and had turned back the cuffs of his frilled dinner shirt. The shirt was open at the neck, and from the disordered state of his hair she thought he had spent some time raking his fingers through it. But it was his expression which even in the moonlight tore at her heart. He looked so strained, so weary, and his eyes held a tortured anguish.

'I am sorry if I woke you, Susannah,' he said, in a low tone. 'I did not intend to do so.'

'But what are you doing in my room, Fernando?' she asked, swallowing convulsively.

He shook his head. 'I do not know. I should ask myself that question.'

'What do you mean?'

He stopped at the side of the bed, looking down at her in the gloom. 'I could say many things, I suppose – give many excuses; but they would all be false. I came because—' He broke off. 'I came because I *had* to. I had to see you. I *needed* to see you to keep my sanity!'

Susannah's lips parted. 'Oh, Fernando,' she breathed huskily. 'What has happened?'

He came down on his haunches beside the bed, reaching for her cold hands and enclosing them inside both of his. Then he said quietly: 'Monica and I have had one of our not infrequent battles, *pequeña*. They are nothing unusual, you understand, but this one was about you!'

Susannah looked down at his hands holding hers. 'Wh – what about me?'

Fernando sighed, bending his head to move his lips against the skin of her fingers. 'I could not permit her to say anything against you. To me, you are something apart from this sordid life of mine. I could not allow her to defame your character.' His fingers tightened on hers.

'I wish to God that I had never married her!'

Susannah quivered. 'You – you must have loved her—'

A shudder passed through him. 'It would have been better for me if I had – if I had some decent thing to cling to,' he muttered harshly. 'But I have none. Monica is married to me, and I am as much to blame for that as she is. More, perhaps.'

'What do you mean? I – I don't understand.'

He glanced up at her momentarily and then resumed his contemplation of her hands. 'How could you? I doubt very much whether anyone, apart from Monica and myself, knows the full story.' He paused. 'I should tell you – I had a brother—'

'A brother?'

'*Si*. His name was Miguel. He was one year older than I am.'

'I see.' Susannah frowned.

'He was not like me, you understand? He was – how shall I say it? – obedient, *si*? He did always what my father wanted. Me ...' he moved his shoulders dismissingly, 'I did not, I preferred my freedom.'

Susannah nodded. She couldn't help but remember what he had told her at the cottage. Of his distress at his mother's death and his subsequent behaviour.

'So,' he continued, 'Miguel stayed at home with my father and Tia Amalia. He was content to do so. He was the elder son. It was expected that some day he would have charge of the vineyards – of the company. I was unimportant. I was permitted to attend the university in England, to travel, to choose any career I wished.' He shrugged. 'The Alvarez vineyards were thriving. My father was a wealthy man.'

'But something happened to change things?'

'*Si*.' He sighed heavily. 'You probably know that the grape which is cultivated to produce wine needs a hot, dry climate. It needs to be picked in the peak of condition when it is neither too sweet nor too bitter. The sun creates sugar in the grape, and a crop too sweet cannot make a fine wine.' He made an impatient gesture. 'It is a knowledge one learns. It is passed down from father to son. But, as I have said, the weather is most crucial to success. Sixteen years ago there was a very wet season. The grapes were ruined, the crop worthless. Everyone lost money. But we were not yet facing disaster.'

'Disaster?'

'*Si*, disaster.' Fernando seemed to find it difficult to go on. Then at last he said: 'The weather affected everyone. But they were all optimistic that the following year we would have a record harvest. Unfortunately, it was not to be. Not for the vineyards of Don Esteban d'Alvarez. The roots of the vines were attacked by a particularly virulent disease. There was nothing we could do about it. The vines had to be torn up and destroyed. New vines were needed, and we could not afford to pay for them.'

Susannah put one of her hands on his head, smoothing the tumbled hair. She had the terrible feeling that she was dreaming all this. That Fernando could not be here, on his haunches beside her bed, relating the circumstances leading up to his marriage to Monica. She felt sure that if she pinched herself hard enough he would disappear.

But she could still hear his voice as he went on: 'Miguel was friendly with a visiting American family in Jerez. Their name was Turner, and Monica was their cousin. She was touring Europe on a prolonged vacation. As you know, she likes to paint a little. She found plenty to interest her in this area. She and Miguel became friends.'

He paused and she could sense the growing tension in him.

'When it became clear that the Alvarez vineyards might have to be sold, my father was desperate. He appealed to Miguel to do something to recover our fortunes. It was known that Monica was a rich woman.' He shook his head. 'All Americans visiting Europe at that time were rich, were they not?' He stroked her wrist. 'Miguel was not unwilling, you understand. There was a Spanish family who possibly expected him to marry their daughter, but my father would rather his son restored the

168

vineyards than keep faith with a family not much better off than ourselves.'

'So – Miguel married Monica!'

'No.' Fernando shook his head again. 'Miguel was killed only a week before their wedding.'

Susannah caught her breath. Now she was beginning to see. If Miguel had died, who but Fernando could save the vineyards?

'But – but didn't Monica – I mean—' Susannah stumbled over the words. 'You – you married her instead, didn't you?'

Fernando nodded. 'You mean, of course, did not Monica mind that it was me and not Miguel?' At her nod, he continued: 'No, she did not mind. At least, not then. I had been away, as I have said. Monica and I had never met until I returned home for my brother's funeral. She was, I suppose – physically attracted to me.'

Susannah sensed what it had cost him to admit that. He was loath to find any excuses for his behaviour.

'So now you can see the ghastly dilemma I was in. My father had never asked anything of me before. I could not fail him.'

'No.' Susannah's voice was quiet.

'But of course it didn't work. Oh, we tried to begin with, but it was useless. Monica and I are simply not suited to one another, but for Marla's sake we maintain appearances.'

'And is that enough?' exclaimed Susannah, aghast.

'No.' His voice was strangled. 'No, of course it is not enough. Not now, at least. Before – before I met you, I did not care. But in London—' He broke off bitterly. 'It would be better if we had never met.'

'You – you told Monica about – about us?'

'No.' Fernando shook his head vigorously. 'No. I could not have borne her vile satisfaction at the news that I was no better than she,' he muttered. '*Cristo*, Susannah, why did you come here? When I thought you had known I was married and had come here to torment me, I pretended I hated you. But when, in your innocence, you declared the truth, I was desperate for you to leave. I was afraid – afraid that if you did not go, *this* might happen!'

He raised tormented eyes to hers, searching her face for some sign that she still felt the same. The haunting sadness of her eyes, the vulnerable curve of her pale cheeks, the parted softness of her lips were too much for him to withstand. With a groan of despair that was compounded of his desire to touch her and the self-loathing it inspired, his hands encircled her throat beneath the neckline of her gown, lingering against the silky swathe of hair loose about her shoulders. He drew her towards him and pressed his lips to the hollow between her breasts where her gown had parted. His touch was probing, gentle, devastatingly destructive to any defence she might try to raise against him. Then he was on the bed beside her, and his mouth was covering hers, gently at first but with ever-increasing passion. Susannah was pressed back among the silken bedcoverings, and in the scented darkness the weight of his body was an added protection against the world outside her room.

'Susannah, Susannah,' he breathed harshly against her throat. 'Forgive me, but I love you so much . . .'

Susannah's arms were around his neck, her fingers were tangled in his hair, and a sensuous lethargy was creeping over her body. Fernando should not be here, and certainly she should not be allowing him to kiss her and caress her as he was doing. But the events of the day had been such that they had weakened her resistance to him, and in those mindless minutes she had no thought of the possible consequences to herself.

But with cruel indifference the intimacy between them was suddenly shattered. The bedroom was brilliantly illuminated as a hand flicked the switch at the door, and Fernando rolled on to his back as Monica came slowly into the room. She was still wearing the orange chiffon gown she had worn earlier, and the inevitable cigarette was between her fingers.

'My *God!*' she muttered disbelievingly, her eyes shifting from Fernando to Susannah and then back to Fernando again. 'Amalia was right. That is the way of it. My

God, no wonder you were so quick to defend our dear governess this evening. Hypocrite! How dare you preach at me when all the time—'

'It's not like that—' began Susannah desperately, holding the neckline of her gown closely to her. But Fernando was rising from the bed and he signalled to her to be silent.

He fastened the buttons of his shirt with deliberate slowness, apparently uncaring of the fury on his wife's face, and walked towards her.

'Before you begin making accusations, Monica, I suggest we continue our confrontation elsewhere—'

'Why? Why should we? Do you want to spare your mistress the sordid details—'

'Susannah is not my mistress!' he muttered violently.

'No? You could have fooled me!'

Fernando's mouth twisted. 'Do not be coarse, Monica!'

'Coarse? What's coarse? I walk in here and find the man who's supposed to be my husband—'

'*Be silent!*' He almost shouted the words. 'Who sent you here? Oh, yes, you mentioned Amalia. It would be her.'

'She's obviously more astute than you had given her credit for being,' remarked Monica coldly. 'How long has this been going on?'

'It has not been "going on",' retorted Fernando grimly. 'What you have just seen was the culmination of a situation you yourself contrived to create!'

'Don't you think it's a little premature?'

Fernando's eyes flashed. 'Susannah and I have known one another for almost three months.'

Monica's lips parted. 'You mean, there was something in what Lucie intimated?'

'As I have no idea what Lucie Castana might or might not have intimated, I cannot answer your question.'

'She said you had shown an exorbitant interest in the girl.'

Fernando made an impatient gesture. 'I see. Did she also tell you that she greeted me one morning in a transparent negligée intended to arouse an interest that was never stimulated?'

Monica dropped the end of her cigarette on the tiles and stamped her foot on it. 'All right, you don't have to tell me about Lucie Castana.' She gave Susannah a brooding look. 'I always thought you were a pretty cool individual. It just shows – looks can be deceiving.'

Fernando raked a hand through his hair. 'I suggest we leave – Susannah – to spend the rest of the night in peace, Monica. We are all tired. We might be tempted to say things we do not mean.'

Monica shrugged her shoulders. 'Just tell me something: exactly what's with you and – and her?'

Fernando heaved a sigh. 'Is that important?'

Monica gasped. '*I* think so. And I'm pretty sure she thinks so, too. Or is this whole scene intended to humiliate *Miss* King into leaving?'

Fernando clenched his fists. 'Very well, Monica. I love Susannah. Is that enough for you?'

'Does she love you?'

'Yes,' Susannah answered abruptly. 'Yes, I love him. But I didn't know he was married when I came here.'

Monica gave her an old-fashioned look. 'Didn't you?' she mocked.

'No, I didn't. How could I?'

'I gather my dear – husband – didn't tell you himself.'

Susannah bent her head. 'No.'

'Typical!' Monica gave a scornful snort. 'Well, Fernando? And what are you going to do about it? Marry the girl?'

Fernando took a step towards his wife and then halted, his jaw taut. 'I suggest you get out of here, Monica!' he muttered, and Susannah thought she had never heard anyone sound more threatening.

Monica merely grimaced. 'Well?' she taunted. 'Why don't you? Marry her, I mean. Then we could all live happily ever after, couldn't we?'

Fernando caught her upper arm in a steel-like grip. 'There is a limit, Monica,' he snarled, 'to what I will take.

Do not tempt me to take you at your word. There might be the small matter of disposing of you first, and who knows, I might find that very enjoyable!'

Although Monica maintained a brave face it was obvious his attitude had intimidated her at last. 'Don't be a fool, Fernando,' she exclaimed, snatching her arm out of his grasp, moving voluntarily towards the door. 'Okay, okay, I'll go. You don't have to twist my arm. You don't even have to come with me. I'm broad-minded!'

Before Fernando could make any retaliatory move she had gone, slipping through the door and allowing it to swing to behind her.

Fernando's shoulders sagged as he looked across at Susannah, pale and trembling on the bed. 'What can I say?' he muttered violently. 'To apologize would be to pretend that I would not do the same thing again given the chance, and I know I would.' He pressed a hand wearily to the back of his neck. 'It seems a pointless euphemism, but I have to say I am sorry for – for the unpleasant scene that has just taken place.'

'Fernando—'

'No, please. Do not say anything. I must go. Who knows, Amalia herself may be waiting at the foot of the stairs.'

'Fernando, you don't have to . . .'

'Oh, yes. Oh, yes, Susannah, I do.' He walked towards the door. 'Good night, *amada*. Try to sleep. Things will look much different in the light of morning.'

Susannah hardly slept at all, but towards dawn exhaustion caused her to lose consciousness for a short period. Even so, she was showered and dressed before Maria appeared with her breakfast at a quarter to eight. The maid showed only mild surprise at the English governess's early rising and there was nothing in her manner to indicate that she knew anything of the events of the night before.

After the maid had left her, Susannah poured herself a cup of coffee and paced about the room drinking it. Her head ached with trying to find solutions to the problems

173

that had robbed her of her sleep, and she determined to leave the *casa* as soon as possible. She couldn't stay now, that much was blatantly obvious, but the knowledge that in all probability she would never see Fernando again was tearing her apart.

But what else could she do? In spite of Monica's callous behaviour, and no matter how much she loved Fernando, she could not spend the rest of her life in the shadows of his, conscious that in all matters of importance Monica had the right to demand his first consideration. What kind of a life would that be, never at peace, never able to bear his children, never to know the day-to-day experiences of bringing up a family. At best it would be a purely selfish arrangement, at worst a constant humiliation to his daughter.

Susannah arrived at the studio at nine o'clock, deciding to tell Marla right away that she would be leaving, but the girl was not there. After waiting around for fifteen minutes, there was still no sign of her and Susannah went down, not without some misgivings, to the room where they usually took morning chocolate with Amalia d'Alvarez. Marla was not there either, but Doña Amalia was, and she looked up without surprise when Susannah entered the room.

'Ah, Señorita King,' she observed with satisfaction. 'I thought you would come here. Are you looking for Marla?'

Susannah was loath to discuss her affairs with Amalia d'Alvarez, but she had no choice other than to tell her that Marla had not turned up for her lessons.

'Marla will not be having any more lessons with you, *señorita*,' said Doña Amalia, putting aside the cloth she had been so meticulously sewing. 'She is returning to the convent.'

'Returning to the convent?' Susannah felt a distinct sense of shock. 'When?'

'I do not think that need concern you, *señorita*. It is my nephew's decision.'

Susannah drew an unsteady breath. 'I see.'

Doña Amalia looked at her steadily. 'You know why,

do you not, *señorita?*'

The hot colour burned in Susannah's cheeks. 'I – I don't know what you mean, *señora—*'

'I think you do, *señorita*. You surely realized you could not remain here after – after everything that has happened.'

Susannah wondered with a sinking heart how much the old woman actually knew and how much she had guessed. It was inconceivable that Fernando should have discussed his affairs with her, and similarly Monica was hardly likely to confide in her arch-enemy. Even so, it was disconcerting to find that one's personal affairs could become common knowledge without any apparent effort.

'As – as a matter of fact, *señora,*' she managed at last. 'I wanted to see Marla for that very reason – to tell her I was leaving.'

Doña Amalia could not hide her delight at this news. 'I am sure her father will already have informed her of his decision, *señorita.*

Susannah's throat was dry. 'Yes. Maybe.' She straightened her shoulders. 'Is – Don Fernando in his study, *señora?*'

'My nephew is not in the *casa, señorita*. He will not be back until this evening.'

That was a blow. She had somehow imagined that today of all days Fernando would make himself available. If, as Doña Amalia had said, he expected her to leave, surely he did not expect her to go without seeing him? Or did he? Wouldn't that perhaps be the kindest way?

Now she moved her shoulders in a confused gesture. 'I – is Señora d'Alvarez available, then? Señora Monica d'Alvarez, that is?'

'I have no knowledge of Señora d'Alvarez' movements, *señorita,*' retorted Doña Amalia coldly. 'Why do you wish to see my nephew or his wife?'

'I feel I should offer my resignation to my employers, *señora—*'

Doña Amalia's relief was evident. 'Is that all? My

dear Señorita King, I can offer your apologies to my nephew and his wife, if indeed such apologies are necessary.'

Susannah looked at the old woman unhappily. She didn't altogether trust her. She had only her word that Fernando intended to dismiss her. Surely she ought to insist upon seeing him before leaving. Doña Amalia seemed overly keen to get her away from the *casa*.

'I really think—' she was beginning, when a shadow darkened the doorway and glancing round Susannah found Monica behind her.

'Well, well, well!' remarked the American woman mockingly, 'what is going on here? Where's Marla? Isn't she having any lessons today?'

Doña Amalia looked furious. 'Señorita King and I were having a private conversation, Monica. I should be grateful if you would leave us to finish it.'

Monica ignored her, touching Susannah's shoulder imperatively. 'Well?' she said. 'Where is Marla?'

Susannah sighed. 'I understand Marla is returning to the convent for lessons—'

'Really?' Monica put a cigarette between her lips. 'Who says so?'

'Monica, please!' Doña Amalia rose from her seat. 'I want to know on whose authority Marla is returning to the convent. Fernando's?'

'Of course it is my nephew's wish,' declared Doña Amalia coldly. 'Señorita King is leaving. That is her decision, not mine.'

'You're leaving?' Monica stared at Susannah in dismay. 'You can't be!'

Susannah was flabbergasted. That Monica should want her to stay on after the scene last night was incredible.

'I'm afraid I must,' she said quietly.

Monica compressed her lips angrily. 'For God's sake – you can't!'

'Leave the *señorita* alone, Monica.' That was Doña Amalia. 'There is nothing for her here.'

'I disagree.' Monica's face was grim. 'Señorita King is

in love with your nephew. Did you know that?'

Doña Amalia clenched her small hands. 'I do not think such matters warrant discussion, Monica—'

'Why? Why not? What if I told you that Fernando was in love with her, too?'

'Monica!' Doña Amalia was pale.

'Well, it's true.' Monica flung herself into an armchair, one leg draped ungracefully over its arm. 'My God, just when I was beginning to think there might be a small chance—' She raised her eyes heavenward. 'Is there no justice?'

Doña Amalia's face looked pinched. 'I wish you would leave us, Monica. There is no point in embarrassing Señorita King unnecessarily. What you are suggesting is impossible and you know it. You will please to go!'

'Oh, yes. That's what you'd like, isn't it? Hide the facts at all costs! Don't let anything mar the image of the unsullied Alvarez family!'

'Monica, I beg of you—'

'You? Begging me? Oh, Amalia, really! Don't you know that you and I passed the point of appeal many years ago when you first discovered about Max—'

'I – I feel faint.' Doña Amalia swayed realistically and judging from her pallor Susannah thought it more than likely that she meant what she said.

Without waiting for Monica to retaliate she hurried forward and lowered the old lady back into her seat, looking down at her with concerned eyes.

'Can I get you anything, señora?' she asked. 'A drink perhaps?'

Doña Amalia fanned herself with her handkerchief. 'I – I – a little Vichy water, perhaps,' she faltered, but Monica sprang to her feet and said:

'Can't you see she's putting it on? She's afraid you'll learn something that hitherto has been kept a family secret.'

Susannah looked from the old señora to the younger woman at her side. 'Then perhaps if it is such a secret I ought not to be told,' she suggested quietly.

Monica's lips twisted. 'Really? Not even if I told you that there is absolutely no reason why Fernando shouldn't marry you?'

CHAPTER TWELVE

Susannah propelled Toni's pushchair through the park, pausing when the little girl caught sight of the ducks on the pond. 'Quack-quacks!' announced Toni, in her babyish treble, and Susannah smiled and knelt down beside her, pointing out the graceful swans who maintained an aloof distance between themselves and their impetuous cousins.

And while Toni was distracted, Susannah sat crosslegged on the grass, her chin cupped on her hands, wondering whether she had made the right decision in accepting the post of English mistress at the nearby comprehensive school in Kennington.

It was almost two months since she had returned from Spain, two months since that dreadful morning when Monica had made her startling announcement.

To begin with, it had been very hard, a series of sleepless nights and tortured days when she had brooded over the things Monica had told her. But gradually things were falling into perspective and she no longer blamed Fernando entirely for what she had gone through. This post, which just happened to be at the school where Margaret's husband, Peter, worked, had unexpectedly become vacant, and they had both urged her to take it and remain with them for the time being.

They had been marvellously kind, Susannah acknowledged, with a warming sense of gratitude. They had not asked a lot of awkward questions, or encouraged her to get another job until she had shown herself ready for it, and gradually, in her own time, Susannah had told them the whole story. In fact, in spite of her earlier antipathy towards Fernando, it had been Margaret who had argued the justification of his actions, and through her Susannah was learning to live with the truth.

But on that morning two months ago, when Monica had blurted out the facts about her and Fernando's marriage, it had seemed the final humiliation. The situation itself was not so uncommon. Monica had been married before. She had thought her first husband dead when she married Fernando, but he had turned up some three years later.

Looking at it now, Susannah could see more clearly the terrible dilemma which faced Fernando then. Married to a woman he did not love, and given the opportunity to be a free agent again, any other man might have been excused for taking the easy way out. But Fernando had not done that. In his happiness lay unhappiness and humiliation for someone else – his daughter, Marla.

Monica had explained that she had been only a teenager when she had married a Jewish boy in New York in the early days of the war in Europe. But soon after their marriage, her husband had become concerned for his family in Poland and against all her appeals had left for his homeland. That had been the last she had heard of him for almost twenty years. She had imagined him beaten and dead, possibly a victim of the concentration camps that had sprung up all over Germany. In fact, he had been imprisoned, but he got out alive without family, home or money. When he had eventually saved up enough to go back to America it had been to find his wife married again and living in Spain. That man, of course, was Max Rosenberg, and Monica's statement had explained Fernando's strange behaviour of the night before. He had not intended that she should learn the truth – for his family's sake he was prepared to live a lie.

Toni was getting restless, and Susannah got to her feet and pushed the chair on through the park. It was a beautiful afternoon in late summer, but already there was a nip in the air and the leaves on the trees were turning to gold. It would be autumn soon, the trees would be bare, and there would be no more walks in the park. She would have charge of a class of almost forty children from vastly different homes and walks of life.

When she arrived back at the house, Margaret met her in the hall in something of a fluster.

'Oh, Susannah!' she exclaimed, 'thank heavens you're home!'

Susannah looked past her down the hall but could see nothing amiss. Frowning, she lifted Toni out of her push-chair and said: 'What is it? What's wrong?'

Margaret made a silencing movement with her hands and Susannah looked even more confused. 'There – there's a visitor for you,' she whispered. 'I think it's your Fernando.'

'What?' Susannah's legs almost gave way. 'You're not serious.'

'I am. I'm sure it's him. A Señor d'Alvarez, is that right?' And at Susannah's nod, she added: 'He's quite a dish, isn't he? No wonder you went a little crazy about him.' Then she realized Susannah was beginning to look pale, and said quickly: 'I'm sorry. I'm only trying to relieve the tension. He's paced up and down my living-room carpet until I'm sure he's worn a hole in it!'

Susannah supported herself against the door jamb. 'But what does he want?' she breathed in a low voice, her eyes wide and disturbed.

'To see you, Susannah!' said a deep voice from the opened door of Margaret's living-room. 'If Mrs. French will permit, we can talk in here.'

Margaret made a deprecative gesture. 'Oh – oh, yes. Go ahead!' she murmured uneasily. 'I – er – I'll be in the kitchen giving Toni her tea, Sue, if you want me.'

Susannah shed the navy parka she had worn over her navy slacks, and pulling down the cream sweater she was wearing with them walked past Fernando into the living-room. She was as nervous as a cat and refused his suggestion that she should sit down.

'Why are you here, Fernando?' she asked, without pre-amble. 'If you have any ideas about taking up where you left off—'

Fernando's face grew strained. Indeed he looked more tired than she had ever seen him and she could not be sure, but she thought he had lost weight.

'You have a right to say that, of course, Susannah,' he said, quietly, 'but that is not why I am here.'

'I can't think what we have to say to one another,' declared Susannah, her voice annoyingly unsteady. 'As far as I'm concerned, it's all over—'

'*Susannah!* Susannah, hear me out! You walked out on me, remember? You did not even wait to see me – to hear what I had to say! It has taken me almost two months to trace you, and now you refuse to listen to me.'

'What is there to say?' exclaimed Susannah, twisting her hands together. 'Your – wife – made everything abundantly clear.'

'I know she did. But I would have hoped – after what had been between us—'

'What had been between us? Just lies, lies and more lies!'

His fists clenched at his sides. 'Is that what you think?'

'It's what I know. You've never taken me into your confidence over – over anything.'

'Susannah, Susannah! How could I tell you about Monica? For years I have lived by a certain code – for years I have forbidden her to reveal the truth to anyone. How could I destroy that code myself? For Marla's sake, I had to remain silent.'

'So why are you here?' Susannah made an involuntary movement. 'There's nothing more to say.'

'Is there not?' Fernando shook his head. 'You will not then return to Spain?'

'Return to Spain?' Susannah stared at him in amazement. 'How could I return to Spain? I have no intention of living in the Casa d'Alvarez as your mistress—'

He reached for her then, his fingers bruisingly hard upon her shoulders. 'Do not dare to suggest such a thing!' he muttered savagely. 'I have never, at any time, given any intimation that that was my intention.'

'Then why are you here? Fernando, it's two months since I left the *casa*—'

'Do you think I do not know that?' His fingers became more cruel. 'They have been the longest months of my life.'

'Fernando, I don't understand—'

'Then let me explain.' He considered her pale face broodingly. 'Monica has gone. I have permitted her to return to her husband.'

'What?' Susannah felt an irresistible fluttering in her stomach. 'But – but how? I mean—'

'Amalia is dead, Susannah. She died the day after your departure.'

'Oh!' Susannah swallowed convulsively. 'I – I'm sorry.'

'Yes. So am I. Amalia was not the kindest of persons, but she had sacrificed her whole life for her brother and his family, and I think it had soured her.'

'I – I didn't realize she had been ill—'

Fernando sighed heavily. 'Amalia was never a strong person. That was why she spent so many hours sitting and sewing – why she appreciated the company of a younger person.'

'Marla?'

'*Si*, Marla.'

'You don't mean – that is – our outings—'

'No, your outings did not upset her unduly. She was jealous, of course, but that was to be expected. I think it was Monica's behaviour that finally . . .' He paused. 'Who knows? Perhaps it was simply her time.'

'Monica's behaviour? You mean – telling me?'

'Oh, no.' Fernando shook his head. 'You left. In Amalia's eyes, that was sufficient. It was Marla.'

'Marla?' Susannah's eyes clouded. 'You mean – Monica told Marla the truth?'

Fernando nodded. 'I am afraid so. It was the day after you left. I had gone to the vineyards. I was still dazed at your departure. I did not know what to do. When I came home there was a terrible row going on. Monica was shouting and screaming and Marla was desperately trying to calm her aunt. But it was useless. Sooner or later, I suppose, it had to come out.'

Susannah shook her head, avoiding his eyes. 'It was my fault, wasn't it?' she murmured unevenly. 'If I had never come to Spain—'

Fernando shook her gently. 'Do not begin to think such

183

things. You did not know that you were coming to my house when you accepted the position Monica offered. You might say it began when we met in London. In any event, it was all for the best.'

'What do you mean?' Susannah looked at him now.

'Marla already knew.'

'What?'

'Oh, yes. Apparently she had overheard Monica talking to Max Rosenberg on the telephone. She is an intelligent girl. It did not take a great deal of deduction on her part to appreciate that if they were married Monica and I could not be.'

'Oh, Fernando!'

He half smiled. 'You look sad. Do not be. Now that Marla knows the truth, there is nothing to fear.'

'But – Monica—'

'Monica left the house before Amalia's funeral. She was, I think, ashamed. But no doubt she will be happy now that she and Rosenberg can make a life together.'

Susannah hardly dared to speculate what this meant to her. 'And – and why have you been looking for me?' she questioned tremulously.

The hands on her shoulders impelled her towards him, his warm male hardness touched her. 'That is an unnecessary question, *amada*. You *know* why. I want you to marry me as soon as it can be arranged.'

Susannah could hardly believe her ears. This afternoon she had gone for her walk with Toni feeling that nothing would ever be the same again. Now Fernando was here, he had told her he loved her, and he was asking her to marry him!

'I – I—' she began confusedly, and then his mouth was on hers and all coherent thought ceased. He held her close against him, moulding her body to his, kissing her and caressing her as if he would never let her go.

'Susannah *mia*,' he groaned against her neck, his body trembling with the tumult of his emotions. 'Tell me you forgive me for what is past. Tell me you love me – that you will marry me.'

Susannah pressed herself against him eagerly. 'Oh, I

love you, Fernando,' she breathed urgently. 'You know I do. And if you want me I'll marry you whenever you say.'

He kissed her again, his mouth bruising her. He was hungry for her and he could hardly bear to let her go. But at last he propelled her away from him and reached into his pocket for his cheroots, putting one between his teeth with unsteady fingers.

Susannah watched him light it with undisguised emotion, and then said: 'You said you had been searching for me. How did you find me?'

Fernando put an arm about her shoulders and drew her down on to the couch beside him. 'You may well ask,' he said dryly. 'It has been almost impossible.'

'Did you contact the Castanas?'

'I did. But they had no forwarding address.' He shook his head. 'Can you imagine how I felt when I discovered this? I was desperate.'

'So what happened?' Susannah was intrigued.

Fernando drew on his cheroot with evident enjoyment. 'Well, I did many things. I contacted all the agencies in London, but I – how do you say it – drew a blank.' He nodded. 'And then I had this brainwave. You had said you were brought up in an orphanage in the north of England, in Yorkshire? You remember?'

'But there must be many children's homes in Yorkshire.'

He half smiled. 'That is why it has taken so long. But eventually someone remembered that you had had a friend who married a schoolteacher called French – and here I am!'

'Oh, Fernando.' Susannah pressed her face against his shoulder. 'If I had never told you about that—'

'I should have been demented.' His eyes darkened passionately. 'Do you think we should call in your good friend and tell her our news?'

'Oh, yes.' Susannah sat up, nodding. But then her eyes clouded. 'Fernando, what about Marla?'

'What about Marla?'

'She may resent me.'

He shook his head. 'I think not.' His hand touched her cheek. 'You know she is very fond of you. She was never very close to her mother. She needs a confidante.'

'I know. But – a stepmother!'

'You will be her mother,' said Fernando definitely. 'Monica – well, Marla will decide about Monica for herself when she is older. Marla is already my daughter. I adopted her when the truth about Rosenberg came to light. Now she will be your daughter, too.'

Susannah got to her feet, reluctant to leave him even for a moment. Then another thought struck her.

'I – I have a job!' she exclaimed. 'I'm due to start at the comprehensive school a week on Monday.'

Fernando's expression darkened for a moment. 'And?'

Susannah's lips curved. 'I suppose I could – withdraw.'

'You had better,' remarked Fernando, with complacent arrogance.

IS THIS THE FIRST TIME

you have read a Mills & Boon paperback? If it is and you have enjoyed reading this story, we would like to take this opportunity of telling you about our books. We believe that we can introduce you to a series of novels which will give you tremendous pleasure.

At present we publish TEN paperbacks on the first Friday of every month and they are obtainable from bookshops, newsagents and department stores all over the world. However, if you should have difficulty in obtaining them from your local stockist our special Reader Service will be only too pleased to help you with your enquiries. The Reader Service carries a complete stock list of over 400 titles published over the last few years together with a large hardback selection. Please write to MILLS & BOON READER SERVICE, P.O. BOX 236, 14 Sanderstead Rd, South Croydon, Surrey CR2 0YG, England* for their complete stock list and magazine – 'HAPPY READING' – (post free).

*Will South Pacific readers please write to MILLS & BOON READER SERVICE, P.O. BOX 958, North Sydney, N.S.W. 2060, Australia.

YOUR ASTRAL GUIDE

Specially written for Mills & Boon readers, this series of paperbacks is a must for every woman who needs to know the facts about the men in her life (husbands, boy-friends and bosses).

YOUR ASTRAL GUIDE

There is one book for each star sign – from Leo to Libra – from Aries to Aquarius.

Unlike other horoscopes – which just give endless pages of predictions – these invaluable little books give vital information how to deal with your man.

 *Do Taureans make good lovers?
 *Are Cancerians too home-loving?
 *Could *you* tame a Leo?
 *What influence does the ascendant sign have on your man's character?

You can find out all this and more. Each book is packed with information, drawings and charts, and only 35p.

---

12 books in the series:

ARIES	LIBRA
TAURUS	SCORPIO
GEMINI	SAGITTARIUS
CANCER	CAPRICORN
LEO	AQUARIUS
VIRGO	PISCES

If you have difficulty in obtaining copies of these books from your local stockist, please write to MILLS & BOON READER SERVICE, P.O. BOX 236, 14 Sanderstead Road, S. Croydon, Surrey CR2 OYG enclosing 35p per book plus 2p for postage and packing. Will South Pacific readers please write to MILLS & BOON READER SERVICE, P.O. BOX 958, North Sydney, N.S.W. 2060, Australia and enclose $1·10 per book plus 30c per order handling.

DID YOU MISS OUR THREE DOUBLES BOOKS?

Violet Winspear
THE STRANGE WAIF
Her memory lost, Lygia's only clue to her identity was a ring mark on the third finger of her left hand – and then she found herself falling in love with a stranger ...

LOVE'S PRISONER
Meeting Lafe Sheridan proved a milestone in Eden's young life, and she knew that no man would ever mean as much to her. But her beautiful sister had more effect on him ... He was rich and lonely, and Gale had always meant to marry a rich man ...

Anne Mather
LORD OF ZARACUS
When Carolyn joined her archaeologist father in Mexico, she found herself immediately in conflict with Don Carlos, who owned the valley where her father was searching for a lost Zapotec city. Don Carlos thought she was as 'a typical product of the permissive society,' and Carolyn let him know that 'I am not one of your peons.' It seemed an inauspicious beginning to their relationship. And yet ...

TANGLED TAPESTRY
Debra knew she was an orphan, but she was twenty-two before she learned who she really was. It was a discovery that was to lead her into a completely new world; the world of films, luxury, glamour – and Dominic McGill.

Anne Hampson
THE AUTOCRAT OF MELHURST
Claire had promised Simon Condliffe that she would stay on in her job as nanny to his small niece as long as he needed her – but she hadn't bargained on falling in love with him, and then having to watch him with his close friend – or was she his fiancée? – Ursula Corwell.

ETERNAL SUMMER
Greece, the land of the gods and of eternal summer; all its beauty spots – Delphi, Athens, the glittering islands; all these were to be part of Marika's daily life – if she agreed to Nikolas Loukas's strange proposal. But would the price be too high?

40p net ($1·40 Aus.) per double book

If you have difficulty in obtaining any of the three books above, please write to **MILLS & BOON READER SERVICE**, P.O. BOX 236, 14 Sanderstead Road, S. Croydon, Surrey CR2 OYG. Will South Pacific readers write to the address on page 191.

MILLS & BOON OLDIES!

20 favourite titles available once again

MILLS & BOON have brought a further 20 of their favourite titles back into print. If you enjoyed reading this book and would like to obtain any of the other titles in this series, please contact your local stockist or in case of difficulty please use the order form overleaf for your requirements, enclosing your remittance.

FREE! Your copy of our MILLS & BOON MAGAZINE – 'HAPPY READING'

Complete the coupon below and send it to MILLS & BOON READER SERVICE, P.O. BOX 236, 14 Sanderstead Road, S. Croydon CR2 OYG, England*, and we will gladly send you, post free, your own copy of our magazine – 'Happy Reading' – which includes a list of the ten new romances we publish every month together with our complete stock list of over 400 Mills & Boon romances.

*Will South Pacific readers please write to: MILLS & BOON READER SERVICE, P.O. BOX 958, North Sydney, N.S.W. 2060, Australia and note all titles are 80c. To cover postage and handling please add 30c per order.

MILLS & BOON OLDIES!

ALL PRICED AT 25p. SEE OVER FOR HANDY ORDER FORM.
PLEASE TICK YOUR REQUIREMENTS.